RETURN OF THE
MORALIS WIFE

RETURN OF THE MORALIS WIFE

BY

JACQUELINE BAIRD

First published in Great Britain 2012
by Mills & Boon, an imprint of Harlequin (UK) Limited.
Large Print edition 2012
Harlequin (UK) Limited, Eton House,
18-24 Paradise Road, Richmond, Surrey TW9 1SR

© Jacqueline Baird 2012

ISBN: 978 0 263 22599 0

Harlequin (UK) policy is to use papers that are natural, renewable and recyclable products and made from wood grown in sustainable forests. The logging and manufacturing process conform to the legal environmental regulations of the country of origin.

Printed and bound in Great Britain
by CPI Antony Rowe, Chippenham, Wiltshire

PROLOGUE

ORION MORALIS—Rion to his friends—impatiently tapped his long fingers on the steering wheel of the powerful sports car. Athens was notorious for traffic snarl-ups, so it was no surprise he was stuck in one. He was going to be late for a damn dinner party he did not want to go to in the first place. It was his father's fault, he mused.

Rion had arrived back from a two-month business trip to the USA late last night. At eight this morning his intercom had been activated and his father had breezed into his apartment.

'To what do I owe this unexpected pleasure?' Rion had asked, and the answer had amazed him.

'I had lunch with Mark Stakis yesterday, and he has agreed to sell his company at a really good price.' He'd quoted a figure. 'How about that?' His dad had beamed. 'I haven't lost my touch yet.'

His father's determination to take over the Stakis shipping line was becoming an obsession. Rion was not involved, but he knew the firm was worth a lot more than what Stakis was asking—the man was giving his business away. But his dad was obviously delighted. He was retiring in the autumn and this deal was to be his last—which was just as well, as his dad was definitely losing his mind if he believed the offer to sell at that price was genuine.

'So what is the catch?' he had prompted dryly.

'Well, Stakis does have a couple of provisos. First, he wants a few shares in the Moralis Corporation instead of more cash. Second, he wants you to marry his granddaughter, so he will know someone of his blood will still be connected to the business that has been his life and his father's before him after he is gone.'

Rion couldn't believe what he was hearing. 'Incredible.' He shook his head. 'I am not marrying any woman for years—if ever—and as for Stakis's granddaughter, it would be a physical impossibility. The man doesn't *have* a grand-daughter. His son Benedict, his wife and teen-age children were killed in a helicopter crash ages ago—or had you forgotten?' he queried seriously.

'No, of course not. It was a tragedy!' his father declared indignantly.

Then his father told him the story. Benedict Stakis had fathered a child with an Englishwoman when his own wife had been pregnant with twins. Stakis had only discovered the existence of his illegitimate granddaughter after his son's death. Apparently Benedict had persuaded the woman to keep quiet in exchange for setting up a trust fund with an English lawyer to provide for the child. Mark Stakis had finally met the girl, Selina Taylor, last September, and now she had finished school she was spending the sum-mer in Greece with him.

'You want me to marry a schoolgirl?' Rion

asked with a laugh, relieved his dad was not going senile. 'You aren't serious?'

'I am serious, and it is not funny. The girl is not a child; she is nearly nineteen. She is staying at Stakis's home in the city and he is holding a dinner party tonight to introduce her to society. We are all invited, so you can meet her and see what you think.'

'No. I don't need to think. Definitely not.'

'At least meet her. This is too good a deal to pass up.'

But pass it up Rion had—adamantly—over and over again. Then his father had brought up some of Rion's past ladyfriends, and a recent episode when Rion had been pictured in a tabloid outside a nightclub arguing with the paparazzi over a married lady who was no better than she should be, and had told him it was time he got himself a good woman instead of the bad he so obviously favoured.

His father had then hinted that he would have to think seriously of delaying his retirement and was not happy at the thought of leaving the business until he knew his son was settled.

His father was not averse to a bit of emotional blackmail... Yet they both knew Rion had, over the past few years, been the driving force behind the diversification from the original Moralis shipping line into the international company it was today. But Rion also knew his father's doctor had warned him after his last heart attack to retire or suffer an early demise. Never mind the fact his stepmother, Helen, would be furious if she had to postpone the world cruise she had planned for his dad's retirement in September.

Finally he had agreed to attend the dinner, but had made it very clear that was all he was promising—and only to humour his father. His dad saw this deal as the finishing touch on a successful career. He might actually succeed in taking over Stakis Shipping, but he would have to do it without Rion marrying some schoolgirl...

The idea of a marriage for business reasons was not something he would ever contemplate—but then he found the idea of marrying for love just as unpalatable. He wasn't convinced the emotion actually existed...

He'd loved his parents, and had thought they'd loved each other. He'd been eleven when his mother had died, and six months later his father had married his secretary, Helen, because she was pregnant. That had hurt Rion, still grieving for his mum. At nineteen he had believed himself in love with Lydia, a stunning society beauty three years older than him. In the year they were together she had vastly expanded his education in the sex department—especially the many and varied ways to please a woman.

Rion had seriously considered asking her to marry him, but swiftly changed his mind when he'd caught her in bed with another woman... Lydia had laughed and suggested he join them, but he had refused, feeling betrayed, and he never did propose. But 'each to his own' was his motto, and they remained friends to this day.

With the benefit of hindsight he realised why Lydia had been such a good teacher!

Now at twenty-eight, Rion had learnt to be

more discerning in his choice of partner. He liked sophisticated women who accepted from the start that all he offered was pleasure for as long as it lasted. He was not into commitment. He had enjoyed a few relationships, but never again imagined he was in love.

The repeated tooting of car horns reminded him where he was and he drove on.

The Stakis house was in the best suburb of Athens. A long drive led up to an impressive entrance portico. Not knowing how many guests were attending, Rion parked at the bottom of the drive so he could make a quick exit. He had a hot date arranged for later with Chloe, a model he had met twice before, and he walked up the drive with a spring in his step that had nothing to do with the dinner party but everything to do with anticipation of ending a couple of months' celibacy...

A maid answered the door and showed him through the rambling old house to where the guests were gathered.

Rion walked into the room and paused when

he saw the girl standing with his half sister, Iris. It had to be the granddaughter—and she was nothing like he had expected and certainly no child, if his body's immediate reaction was anything to go by. Selina Taylor had a knock-out body, and he had to fight to control the pleasurable hardening in his groin area at the sight of her before moving on.

She was about five feet six, with full, firm breasts, a narrow waist, slim hips and fabulous legs—all perfectly displayed by the short emerald-green designer gown she wore and the sexy stiletto sandals.

Up close she was stunning. Her hair was reddish gold, its curls cut short to frame the perfect oval of her face. Her features were even and her complexion as pale as cream—when she wasn't blushing, he amended, which she did rather a lot, he realised as the evening progressed.

But even scarlet-faced she was still lovely. Her expressive eyes fascinated him—big and cat-like, and the most incredible colour: hazel, or amber with a hint of green was as near as he could get.

When she laughed they gleamed golden, and when she glanced his way they widened and she looked at him almost in awe—which he found flattering and incredibly arousing.

She had an innocence about her, and a lack of artifice that was totally genuine, Rion was sure. And he should know. He had met enough women who tried to play the innocent but with eyes as hard as stone.

'So, how long have you been learning Greek, Selina?' he asked her over dinner, wanting to know more about her. He didn't question why...

He was stunned by her reply. She already spoke Italian and French, and had been learning Greek since meeting her grandfather, but she specialised in Chinese and Arabic and was going to university in the autumn.

She was definitely bright—and yet oddly naive. Rion was an experienced man of the world, used to the attention of women, and was well aware of Selina's interest in him as the conversation flowed around the table. Under any other circumstances he would have pursued the mutual sexual attraction, but Selina was strictly out of bounds.

For all her stunning looks she obviously had little experience of men.

Coffee was served, and with his usual iron resolve Rion dismissed Selina from his mind. He took a sip or two of coffee and then swiftly drained his cup. Pushing back his chair, he got to his feet. He thanked Mark Stakis for dinner and made the excuse of a conference call booked at his apartment from the USA.

'Shame you are so pushed for time, but don't let us delay you.' Mark Stakis smiled at him. 'In fact take a shortcut through the garden—it is quicker that way.' Turning to his granddaughter, he said, 'Selina, show Rion the pathway to the drive. It will save him time.'

Of course the girl agreed and rose to her feet. Rion was amazed at how obvious the old man was being, but he couldn't say anything. Instead he followed Selina down the steps from the terrace to the garden path. The poor girl hadn't a clue Mark Stakis was trying to marry her off...

'Steady, Selina.' Rion reached for her arm as she caught the killer heel of one shoe in the decorative paving. 'I am not in as much of a hurry that I want to see you break your lovely neck.' Running his hand down her arm, he clasped her hand. Moving on, he said smoothly, 'So tell me, Selina, how do you like staying in Greece with your grandfather? It must be a lot different from the life you lead in England.'

'There is no comparison.' she said. 'He lives in such splendour.' Glancing up at him, she added, 'In fact I was amazed to discover I *had* a grandfather, and even now I still find it hard to believe.'

She smiled and made no attempt to free her hand from his, and as they walked down the dimly lit garden path, with a little prompting from Rion, she told him all about herself. Her mother was dead and she lived with her Aunt Peggy whom she had known all her life. She had been to continental Europe before, but last Christmas had been her first visit to Greece.

Rion found himself feeling sorry for Selina.

She'd had a mother who had denied her knowledge of her father, a father who had ignored her, and now a grandfather who had befriended her for his own reasons. He looked into her big golden eyes, then down to the soft pink mouth, and suddenly it wasn't sorrow he felt but an overwhelming compulsion to comfort her...kiss her...just once...

He slipped his hands around her waist and drew her gently against him. Lowering his head, he brushed her full lips in a tender kiss. He had meant it to be brief, but the taste of her was instantly addictive. He felt her tremble as he coaxed her lips apart to accept the subtle penetration of his tongue. She swayed against him, her arms wrapping around his neck and her body pressed against the lean, hard length of him.

Rion knew he should stop, but he was enchanted by her taste, her tentative touch, the unconsciously sinuous movement of her body against his, and was reluctant to let her go. Finally, painfully aroused, he drew in a deep, shuddering breath and curved his hands around her shoulders, putting some space between them. He held her for a long moment until his breathing returned to normal, and saw her dilated pupils, the sensual longing in her eyes that she could not disguise. He knew he had to see her again.

Selina was so sexy, and yet so naive. He had an urge to protect her…along with a more basic urge—which of course he knew he must deny, he told himself piously.…

The date he had lined up for after the dinner party was a disaster. Chloe would never speak to him again. He had taken her to a nightclub and then back to her home. Refusing her offer of coffee with a kiss on the cheek, he had left her at the door.

CHAPTER ONE

THE blistering heat of the July day had faded to a bearable level as the luxury yacht glided into the harbour of the Greek island of Letos just before midnight.

Orion Moralis—tall, dark-haired, dark-eyed, and with a dark frown on his handsome face—the powerful, and some would say ruthless, owner of the vast Moralis Corporation—walked down the stairs from the bridge and onto the main deck. Casually dressed in combat pants and an open-necked black shirt, he paused for a moment to look at the assortment of buildings surrounding the harbour. The church tower held centre stage in the only village on the island, where Mark Stakis lived. *Had* lived, he amended with a shrug of his broad shoulders. Though as far as Rion was concerned the man had been dead to him for years.

His yacht, with a crew of seven, was fitted with state-of-the-art technology and had been heading for the coast of Egypt for a rare three-week break. Rion had planned to combine essential work with a cruise and a diving holiday. He had heard the news that Stakis was dead and had had no intention of going to the man's funeral—but yesterday morning he had received an informative e-mail from Stakis's lawyer, Mr Kadiekis, requesting his presence. He had diverted the yacht midway across the Mediterranean to get here—his trip cut short before it had started.

Rion strolled across the deck and stopped at the rail to glance down at the harbour to where a sailor was securing the yacht to its berth. He was impatient to get ashore; he needed to stretch his legs and shake of the restlessness that had plagued him for months—a major factor in his decision to take a break from his hectic work schedule. The restlessness had increased considerably after the news Mr Kadiekis had given him...

Amazingly Mark Stakis hadn't changed his will in years, and the knowledge had brought memories Rion had thought dead and buried to the surface with a vengeance.

Six years ago he had married Stakis's grand-daughter Selina Taylor—and what a mistake *that* had been. Rion rarely if ever made mistakes—in business or in his private life—and it had been a huge blow to his ego when his young wife had betrayed him. For a second black fury blazed through him at the memory. Then abruptly he turned from the rail, and with the gangway in place walked down onto dry land.

Breathing deeply of the night air, Rion walked the length of the harbour away from the lights and onto the beach, enjoying the stillness of the night. The further he walked the more the anger the thought of his ex-wife had aroused in him ebbed away, and he began to relax. He listened to the soft sound of the waves against the shore as he strolled around the headland and through the trees, and realised he had reached the Stakises' private beach.

He stopped for a moment and looked at the sprawling white villa set on the hillside. A single light shone from the building, dimly illuminating the elegant terraces trailing down to the shore. A retaining wall with a gate gave access to the beach and he glanced, around wondering if there was any security. Suddenly the gate opened.

Rion's dark eyes narrowed on the white ghost-like figure that appeared thirty feet away, then widened on the very obvious feminine form... certainly neither ghost nor Security.

He stepped swiftly back into the shadow of the trees as the light of the moon illuminated the woman, jogging over the sand, the white robe she wore flying out behind her.

Selina. It had to be...

Rion stiffened, every muscle in his body tense. Although he'd had prior knowledge that she would be here it was still a shock to see her. The woman had some nerve. It was common knowledge that from the day she had returned to England after their divorce her grandfather had cut off all contact with her. But Rion wasn't surprised. The scent of money was a big lure, he thought cynically.

He stood motionless, his dark eyes narrowed intently on his ex-wife. She obviously thought she was alone as she shrugged off the robe and let it drop to the sand, pausing for a long moment and looking out to sea, a minuscule white bikini her only covering. It was definitely Selina—but not quite as he remembered her. The short, strawberry-blonde hair was now long, swept back in a ponytail that fell midway between her shoulder blades, and as for the rest...

Rion's breath caught in his throat, his eyes darkening in primitive male appreciation and his body hardening as she pulled the tie from her hair to let it fall in shimmering waves down her back. Then, tilting her face to the night sky, she stretched and raised her arms above her head as though in some kind of pagan worship to the moon. Incredibly, she was even more attractive than he remembered, her body toned and shapely. She was a modern-day Eve—temptation personified.

The pale silver light gleamed on high, firm breasts, the shadowed indentation of her tiny waist and the sensual curve of her hips, and he could not take his eyes off her.

Then, as he stared, enthralled by her beauty, she ran forward and leapt, her back arching in a graceful curve as she dived into the sea.

Fascinated he watched her slender arms scything through the water with barely a ripple as she swam out to sea. *Too far out.* The worrying thought hit him, and suddenly she slid beneath the waves. With a knee-jerk reaction Rion stepped forward. But she reappeared an instant later and he faded back into the shadows, his heart pounding, and watched as she changed to a butterfly stroke and drew near the shore. She stilled to float gently on her back, her arms and legs outstretched, like some star nymph of the sea.

Rion had never seen anything more erotic in his life.

She spun a few times, like a whirling dervish playing in the water, and finally walked out of the sea and strolled back up the beach. Reaching for her robe, she slipped it on and looped the belt around her waist. She lifted her hands and, tilting back her head, swept the long mass of her hair back from her face. She paused for a moment.

Fiercely aroused, Rion wanted her with a hunger that disturbed him. Obviously he had been too long without a woman, he reasoned. For a moment he had trouble remembering how long—months, he realised in surprise. Well, that was about to change—and he knew exactly who with…

His eyes raked over Selina, a predatory light in their darkening depths.

He must have made some movement, because her head had turned in his direction as though she sensed his presence. It crossed his mind to walk out and confront her. But the time was not right. It was her grandfather's funeral in a few hours. He could wait…

Selina owed him. Not so much money—though that was obviously the reason for her appearance at her grandfather's funeral, as she was the old man's only relative.

Narrow-eyed and aching with frustration, he watched as she slowly scanned along the treeline where he stood. He held his breath, then let it out slowly when, after what seemed like an age, she finally shook her head and turned to walk away.

His eyes glittered with a ferocious light as he fought to crush the sexual hunger that had hit him like a thunderbolt. Once he had believed Selina was a poor little innocent, with no parents and no one to care for her and a grandfather who had his own agenda. He had felt sorry for her. But not for long. Less than four months after they had met he'd married Selina and she had betrayed him…

Rion had cut her out of his life and his mind. Selina had been dead to him from that moment on. But when he'd heard she was to be here, and he had been gifted a way to make her suffer in a monetary sense—strip her bare for her betrayal—he had decided to do so. But now a much more satisfactory scenario came to mind. His lips curled and there was an anticipatory gleam in his dark eyes. A female companion was a sexual necessity for a relaxing holiday— and who better than Selina? He would strip her bare, all right, and sate himself in her lush body once and for all…

The moment of reckoning had been a long time coming, but now it had. He was going to have Selina again—not tonight, but soon, very soon. They would have the honeymoon he had once planned and never taken. She owed him that much at least. She had fooled him once with the shy, blushing virgin act, and he had treated her with kid gloves for the short time they were married. But she had soon shown how devious she really was—especially when it came to their divorce. This time it would be on his terms. The gloves were off…

* * *

Selina had walked out of the sea and swept back her hair with a smile on her lips, feeling refreshed and at ease, her eyes on the night sky. She'd stiffened as she recognised the constellation of Orion, directly above her. In Greek mythology he was a great huntsman of charm and beauty who on his death had been placed by the gods in the constellations of the sky.

Nothing like the Orion *she* had known, who had all the charm of a rattlesnake, Selina thought scathingly.

She glanced down and along the beach to the distant lights of the harbour, then back towards the trees, and suddenly the hairs on the back of her neck stood on end. She had the strongest feeling someone was watching her. Not the stars—she wasn't a fanciful teenager any more…

Maybe swimming in the middle of the night had not been such a great idea, but the pressure of the past few days had finally got to her, and she hadn't been able to sleep for the heat… Well, that was what she blamed her agitation on, rather than face her grandfather's death and the painful memories returning to Greece had evoked.

Selina could remember with blinding clarity the first time she'd met her grandfather, and the start of a fairy-tale life that had quickly turned into a nightmare.

She'd had a happy childhood with the mother she had loved—a beautiful, dramatic and vibrant woman, a trained opera singer—and her Aunt Peggy, whom she adored. She wasn't really her aunt, but a babysitter-cum-housekeeper—as she had realised when she was about five.

Her mother had told her that her father was dead, and for years Selina had accepted that. So it had come as an enormous shock when, in the September after she turned eighteen, she'd met Mark Stakis—an elderly Greek who had said he was her grandfather and told her the true story of her birth.

His son, Benedict Stakis, was Selina's biological father, and he had died with his family in a tragic accident. Mark Stakis had only learnt of the existence of Selina after his son's death…

It had hurt Selina deeply to realise her mum had always known that Benedict Stakis was alive. But in return for a house, and a guarantee to pay for Selina's upkeep until she was twenty-one, her mum had signed a contract to keep his identity secret from everyone—including her daughter...

Sighing, Selina began walking back to the villa. In the seven years since she had met her grandfather life had taught Selina a lot. She had seen some of the terrible things people were forced to do just to live in this world, and she no longer judged her mother quite so harshly for doing what she had done to ensure a good life for her daughter.

God, she had been so naive when she had met her grandfather, Selina thought, entering the villa and closing the door behind her. She had spent Christmas with him, here in this house. She glanced around the huge if somewhat tired-looking reception hall. But it had been what had happened the next time she'd visited Greece that had haunted her for years. Not any more. She was her own woman now and intended to remain that way.

In her experience good men were in a minority, and ruthlessly ambitious immoral men were in the ascendancy in today's world. She only had to remember her younger self and the night she'd met Orion Moralis to confirm her view, she thought, letting her mind slip back to the past...

She had been so excited to be back in Greece for a second time, and she'd been staying in her grandfather's house in Athens. He had held a dinner party, inviting the Moralis family.

Selina had been introduced to Helen Moralis and her daughter, Iris, a few days earlier, and they had been kind enough to take her around the sights and shops. They were there, with Paul Moralis, the husband and father.

Orion, the son, had arrived late, and Selina had taken one look at him and thought 'tall, dark and handsome' could have been coined for him. He had smiled and talked to her, his twinkling dark eyes mesmerising her, and with every passing minute she had fallen deeper under his spell.

Finally, when dinner was over, he'd said he had to leave early to take a conference call. Her grandfather had told her to lead Rion out through the garden because it was quicker.

She had stumbled on the garden path in the high heels Iris had convinced her to buy, along with the daring green dress she'd been wearing, and Rion had caught her. He had kept hold of her hand and talked to her, charmed her, and finally kissed and caressed her.

She had fallen headlong in love with him.

Even now, years later, the memory made Selina shiver—with revulsion, she told herself. The only person being led down the garden path that night had been her, she had realised bitterly a few months later.

Straightening her shoulders, she glanced around the silent house and walked up the grand staircase to her bedroom. Tomorrow was her grandfather's funeral. She had to stay strong to get through the day. As Anna had said, it was up to Selina, his only relative, to ensure his funeral was perfect—as befitted a man of his great stature.

Personally, Selina wasn't convinced he had been great. But when Anna, his housekeeper—the one person who had befriended Selina in the past and the only one she had kept in touch with since leaving Greece—had called to say he was seriously ill, and had asked Selina to come immediately, she hadn't been able to refuse. Now she was glad she had arrived two days before her grandfather had died. They'd had a chance to talk and make a sort of peace with each other.

Reconciled with her grandfather, however briefly, Selina had agreed with Anna's suggestion that she stay and act as hostess to the guests that were expected for the funeral. Now was not the time to be reliving painful memories of the past—if ever…

Rion Moralis waited until he saw Selina disappear through the garden gates and reappear walking up the terraces that led to the villa.

There was a shaft of light as she opened the door of the house and vanished again. She was obviously home safe.

Turning, he strolled back along the beach the way he had come, remembering the first time he'd set eyes on Selina. Thinking about it now, as he rounded the headland and saw the lights of the harbour, Rion smiled grimly. That fatal day had been the start of the train of events that had led to his disastrous marriage.

Selina had not been the usual kind of woman he was attracted to, but that had not stopped his body reacting instantly the moment he saw her. She had blushed when they were introduced, but in conversation over dinner it had become obvious she was a bright young woman.

Later, when she'd walked with him through the garden to his car, against his better judgement he had kissed her. With hindsight he realised he had behaved like the teenager Selina actually had been, letting his body's desire have its way. He'd kissed her again and she had responded with eager naivety, confessing she had never been kissed before—which had only inflamed him more. She hadn't tried to stop him when he'd trailed his hand down her throat, traced the creamy curves of her breasts, his fingers slipping beneath the fabric of her dress to tease the small, pink nipples…

Damn it… He was hard again at the memory. He had never felt such an uncontrollable urge for sex with a woman before or since—and it had to stop.

He had proposed to her on this very island soon after they'd met, and had married her on the seventeenth of July in the local church—to the delight of his father and Mark Stakis.

Later, Rion had cynically decided that given the circumstances of their meeting and his opinion of the female sex, he hadn't been so much surprised as angry when, nine weeks into the marriage, he had returned from a business trip early in the morning on the day of her nineteenth birthday, wanting to surprise her with a diamond pendant he had commissioned specially for her and with arrangements made for a belated honeymoon in the Seychelles.

He had surprised her, all right—with a man. Leaping out of her bed. Not a man—more a boy...

When he'd been able to see through the red haze of fury that had engulfed him, naturally he had thrown her out and informed his lawyer to instigate divorce proceedings immediately. He had neither seen nor spoken to her since.

But he *had* been surprised, and absolutely furious, when he had discovered just how bright the supposedly shy Selina was when it came to their divorce...

She had refused to sign papers admitting adultery for a swift no-contest divorce in front of his lawyer and her grandfather, then returned to England and consulted a lawyer of her own— the father of her friend Beth, both of whom had been guests at the damned wedding!

Her lawyer had then had the audacity to inform Rion's lawyer that Selina would consent only to a no-fault divorce. Otherwise she would meet him in open court. The devious little witch had intended to cross-petition, citing Rion's adultery with various women!

His lawyer had advised him that although Selina had little chance of winning it would be wiser to accept her offer and avoid the publicity a court case would arouse. Her lawyer had evidence to support Selina's case: video clips of Rion from gossip websites.

One was of him with Chloe in the nightclub, the same night he had met Selina. Chloe was quoted as giving him a score of four out of ten for his sexual ability. A woman scorned, he thought ruefully. Another was of Rion arguing with a photographer outside a club while Lydia, who was now married to Bastias, an influential Greek banker, looked on, plus a couple of other women Rion barely recalled meeting and certainly had not bedded.

Rion had had no choice but to agree with his lawyer—though it had infuriated the hell out of him to do so... Grimly he had conceded that the internet was great for business but a thousand times more lethal than the paparazzi when it came to one's private life. Even now it enraged him that he'd been outwitted by a faithless teen-age wife…

He had blanked her from his mind. He'd been a free man again and had got on with his life, expanding his business empire. But now, after hearing from Kadiekis and seeing her tonight, she filled his mind again as he walked back to his yacht.

Making for his cabin, he stripped off and took a long, cold shower…

CHAPTER TWO

SELINA kept her head bowed as the coffin was lowered into the ground. Mark Stakis was the grandfather she had never known existed until she was eighteen—and now, seven years later, he was dead.

Most of the villagers had turned up for the service, and a lot of the social elite from Athens had arrived by helicopter. She felt as if the eyes of every single one of them were on her, watching and waiting to see if she would break down and cry, as a good granddaughter should. But then she had never been a good granddaughter. She was the bastard from England who had been kept secret for years.

Even after her mum's death when she was fifteen she had lived in blissful ignorance of the truth of her birth for three more years. After meeting her grandfather she hadn't known what to think any more. The certainties in her life had been shaken. Maybe that was why she had leapt so hastily into marriage? she thought. Not that it mattered now. Her grandfather had been kind to her in his way, she supposed, and before he died he had said he was sorry, he had done what he'd thought was best for her…

What a horrendous mistake *that* had been…

With hindsight she should have known. On discovering the truth about her father and the death of his family she should have realised she was the only relative Mark Stakis had left—and given his state of health—was ever likely to have.

Talk about a tragedy, Selina mused. Rich Greeks seemed to have a predilection for them. More money than most people could ever dream of and what good did it do? When he could have built a good relationship with Selina, once she'd got over the secrets and lies she had grown up with, her grandfather had wrecked any possibility of it happening with more secrets and lies.

If only he had been honest from the beginning, she thought sadly, a tear sliding down her cheek.

The priest's voice broke into her reverie and she lifted her head, bent and picked up a handful of earth and dropped it on the coffin.

Standing by the priest, Selina accepted the condolences of the guests as they filed past, and invited everyone back to the villa. Finally, with a supreme effort of will, she forced herself to look coolly up at the last guest. She had glimpsed his presence at the back of the church as she had followed the priest out. Shock had slammed through her for a moment, then determinedly she had chosen to ignore him, but now she had no choice…

Orion Moralis—her ex-husband—a man she had hoped never to see again in her life…

He looks older, was her first thought, *and more impressive than ever* was her second. Six feet two with thick black hair. Her glance skimmed over his hard, handsome face and down to his broad shoulders. He was wearing a black silk

suit, a white shirt and black tie, and in the siz-
zling summer sun he still managed to look cool.

Rion was the type of man she actively
disliked—arrogantly sure of himself and never
listening to anyone. As she knew to her cost. A
man used to ordering others around, getting his
own way. And yet there was something about
the enigmatic dark eyes, the sardonic arch of the
black brows, the curl of his lip, the jut of his jaw
that was compellingly attractive. Sexy… But not
to her. Not any more.

'I'm sorry for your loss, Selina,' his deep, dark
voice drawled, and she would have had to be
deaf not to hear the sarcasm in his tone!

'Thank you,' she responded equally insin-
cerely, and stiffened as two strong hands curved
firmly around her shoulders and pulled her close
to his long body.

Shockingly, the strength, the warmth and the
scent of him reached out to her, and a flicker of
heat ignited low in her belly. He bent his dark
head and in that fractured moment she knew he

was going to kiss her. His lips brushed one pale cheek and then the other.

'What do you think you are doing?' she snapped, angry at her involuntary reaction to him.

'Protecting my business interests,' he mouthed against her ear. 'A death can cause trouble in a company if there is a hint of disagreement between shareholders—and your grandfather was a shareholder.'

How typical, Selina thought, the warmth vanishing. She almost laughed out loud, but didn't dare. She had a horrible feeling that after the emotional upheaval of the past few days she would end up crying.

Taking a step back, she shrugged his hands from her shoulders. 'You have not changed,' she said with a shake of her head. 'Always business first—last and always.'

'Not always. The last time I was on this island was the day I married you—and I didn't have business on my mind then,' he drawled.

Selina glared at him—and wished she hadn't.

The latent desire in his dark eyes reminded her of another time, and for a moment she could not look away. But as he continued to speak her problem was solved.

'But you are right, Selina, business is my passion—which is lucky for you. You are about to become a wealthy woman…but then you probably already know that.'

He was still the overwhelmingly arrogant chauvinistic pig she remembered—and she also remembered something else.

'All I know is that for a man who the last time we met swore never to see or speak to me again you are remarkably visible and verbose,' she said mockingly, and had no trouble walking away to join the priest.

She thanked him for the service and strolled with him to a waiting limousine. It was a mile from the church to the villa, and she was glad to escape into the air-conditioned interior of the car. She was hot and angry and she could not be sure it was just the sun…

From the first time she'd set eyes on him Rion

had made her blush and a whole lot more… But never again she vowed. She knew him for what he really was. Most men would be content to be born with wealth, but not Rion. He was a ruthless, manipulative devil who would step over anyone who got in the way of his driving ambition for more wealth and power. Since they had parted she had seen men a whole lot worse than Rion, she conceded, but with the same driven need.

Men who pursued their own selfish desires to the detriment of others and who were instrumental in the choices she had made in her own life…

Selina had a point, Rion conceded, a wry smile twisting his lips as he watched her walk away. Her shapely bottom swayed temptingly beneath the tight black skirt of the elegant sheath dress she wore. She still had a fantastic pair of legs, he noted as her dress rode up to her thighs as she slid into the backseat of a limo, and she had obviously learned how to walk in high heels. Selina had always been a lovely girl, but now she had fulfilled her potential and matured into a stunningly elegant and beautiful woman.

Rion's resolve hardened as he began the walk to the Stakis villa. When he had held her he had seen in the darkening depths of her expressive eyes that for all her outrage Selina wasn't immune to him. The attraction was still there.

Yes, seducing Selina would give him incredible satisfaction. Every rampant hormone in his body was telling him that. As would her final surrender and her humble apology for having the colossal nerve to try and tarnish his good name by suggesting they contest their divorce in an open court.

The memory of the action Rion's lawyer had first suggested he pursue—labeling Selina an adulteress for the rest of her life—conveniently escaped him, but while he walked towards the Stakis home his determination to make sure *Selina* didn't escape him grew with every step he took…

Selina sensed the moment Rion walked into the room—because however much she tried she couldn't quite dispel the disturbing awareness that arose within her whenever she was in his presence. And she wasn't the only one, she recognised.

Dynamic and strikingly attractive, he bore a sophisticated air of wealth and power combined with a raw animal magnetism. Men and woman alike could not help but recognise it, and the momentary pause in the chatter of conversation confirmed it.

The noise and laughter soon resumed and she thought dryly that the Greeks certainly knew how to enjoy themselves.

After pretending to listen to Mr Kadiekis, her grandfather's lawyer, waxing lyrical about his brilliant son who had just passed his law exams, she excused herself, with the explanation that she needed to check on the staff. She wove her way through the guests with a pleasantry to some and an acceptance of condolences to others.

Selina had almost made it to the kitchen when Rion stopped in front of her, blocking her way through the crowd of people.

'You are looking flushed, Selina. I saw you talking to your grandfather's lawyer. Anticipation getting to you?' he prompted, and looked at her with a hint of mocking arrogance in his expression.

The smirk and his cynical implication that she was here for what she could get from her grandfather's death got to her. Tossing back her head, she let her eyes clash with his. 'I don't know what you are trying to imply, and I don't want to know. You will have to excuse me. I need to check the kitchen,' she said, coolly polite.

'No, you don't. You simply want to avoid me. And I have to wonder why,' he replied, with the sardonic arch of one black brow.

Selina tilted her chin and looked up at him. 'We are divorced—have been for years, remember?' she prompted, sarcasm evident in her tone. 'And, to be blunt, I don't like you.' She'd told him straight—now he would leave her alone.

'There was a time when you did,' he said, and the reminiscent gleam in the dark eyes that met hers made her heart miss a beat. 'Once we were as close as two people can be, Selina…a hell of a lot more than once,' he teased softly.

For a second, a vivid image of their bodies entwined flashed in her mind, and she wished it had not.

'True, we parted badly, but I forgave and forgot years ago. Surely now we can be friends?'

Friends? Rion had to be joking after the way he had treated her. She recognised the basic all-masculine gleam in his eyes—she had seen it in many a man's eyes in the years they had been apart. She wasn't a naive teenager any more, and she knew it wasn't a friend he wanted. But she couldn't prevent the sudden tightening in her chest or the throb of her pulse. Anger, she told herself, and swallowed hard. She was unable to speak for a moment, or tear her gaze away.

Rion took a glass of wine from the tray of a passing waitress and handed it to her.

'Here—join me in a drink for old times' sake. As I recall we had our moments…' he drawled, his gaze roaming brazenly over her body.

Selina knew exactly the moments he was referring to. Without thinking she took the glass. Their fingers brushed and a shiver snaked down her spine. Quickly she raised the glass to her lips and took a sip. Long-buried memories were re-surfacing in her mind. The connection she had felt the moment she saw him, their first kiss, their lovemaking, his tanned, naked body, all muscle and sinew… He had been like a Greek god to her, with his thick, silky black hair and his soulful eyes with their curtains of black lashes…

Damn—what was she thinking? Selina blinked. There was nothing soulful about Rion. Soulless, more like. She took another gulp of wine. Why on earth was she recalling the good times they had shared when the bad had far out-numbered everything else?

Selina had been married to Rion for eight weeks when his father had retired and set off with Helen on a world cruise. They had moved from Rion's apartment to stay at the family home and watch over his half sister Iris for a the last couple of weeks of her summer vacation, and then see her safely returned to the international school she attended in Switzerland. During the second week, Rion had gone to Saudi Arabia on business.

Iris had asked if she could invite some friends over on the Thursday evening, for a farewell party before she returned to school. Rion had not been due back until the Friday night, so Selina had agreed—she hadn't seen any harm in Iris having a little party.

Selina could still recall every minute detail of the whole mortifying scene when Rion had returned unexpectedly very early the next morning. Hearing her name called, she had woken from a deep sleep to glimpse a half-naked man dashing out of her room. Rising up on her elbows, she'd seen Rion standing at the foot of the bed, his dark eyes blazing with fury, rage etched in every line of his hard face.

'Rion…' She'd shaken her head in confusion. 'What…? Who was that…?'

'Your lover,' he snapped, his eyes as hard as jet, his face suddenly an expressionless mask.

'Get up, clean up and get out. The marriage is finished. I never want to see or speak to you again.'

'You can't mean that—this is some ghastly mistake!' she'd cried.

But it had been no mistake. He'd spun on his heel and left without another word.

She remembered the utter humiliation she had felt when she'd realised Rion had instructed the staff to escort her from the house before noon and ordered a car to send her back to her grandfather in disgrace—the adulteress wife on her nineteenth birthday, of all days. She'd tried to get in touch with Rion but it had been hopeless. As he had sworn on the morning he threw her out, he wouldn't see her, wouldn't listen and wouldn't speak to her.

The final disillusionment had come a day later, when she'd managed to meet Iris. Selina had told Iris she was sure she had not had sex with the boy, Jason, as that evening she had gone to bed early, with a couple of painkillers for cramps. The next morning, confused and in tears after

Rion's dismissal of her, she had stumbled into the shower and realised the feminine protection she wore was still firmly in place.

Iris had just laughed and said she knew anyway. Then she had admitted that Jason, the neighbours' gardener, was her boyfriend. After Selina had gone to bed the rest of them had continued drinking. Iris had told Jason to wait until everyone had left and then give her ten minutes before following her up to her bedroom, the second on the left. Unfortunately the idiot had taken the second on the right, ended up in Selina's bed and passed out.

Jason had told her the sound of footsteps in the hall had awakened him, and when he'd seen a redhead instead of Iris's black hair on the pillow next to him he'd been horrified. Panicking, he had leapt out of bed, pulling on his pants, and had run for the door just as Rion had walked in. Head down, he hadn't stopped running until he was out of the house.

Selina had begged Iris to tell Rion the truth but she'd flatly refused, saying her life would not be worth living if she did. Rion would tell her parents and she would be grounded for months—if not years. To justify her refusal Iris had told Selina that Rion had already arranged to take her back to school tomorrow and fly on from Switzerland to the USA, for an unspecified length of time. Selina would be better off going back to England and to university, she'd told her, and getting on with her life. Because Rion didn't really love her. He had only married her to seal a business deal with her grandfather.

Iris had overheard her parents talking about it when they'd thought she was asleep in the back of the car on the way home from Selina and Rion's engagement party at a deluxe Athens hotel. She'd added that Rion would never be faithful anyway, because much as she adored her brother he was a confirmed womaniser. To prove her point she'd got out her laptop and shown Selina some of the pictures and comments Rion's female friends had posted on social websites.

Reading what other women said about their relationships with Rion had been mortifying. One had been a posting by a woman called Chloe, pictured with Rion in a dimly lit club. The date was a date that was engraved on Selina's mind: the night she had first met Rion and he had kissed her. He had lied even then! He had not hurried off after dinner for a conference call but to meet this woman…

But what had finally convinced Selina was a shot of Rion arguing with a photographer outside a nightclub with a woman named Lydia looking on. Iris had told her that Rion had been in love with Lydia, and wanted to marry her years ago. But she had married a banker, Bastias, instead.

Sickeningly, Selina had realised, that Rion had introduced her to this Lydia and a woman friend in a restaurant on one of the rare occasions he had taken her out to dinner. Her heart, already cracked, had finally shattered into a million pieces, her love destroyed and turned to dust.

She'd been left devastated, but angry with herself for being such a fool, and on returning to

England Selina had determined to get back at Rion through his arrogant pride. Amazingly, she had succeeded—and though it had not mended her broken heart it had gone a long way to restoring her confidence, Selina thought now as she drained her glass of wine. She was a much stronger woman for the experience, and she had no need to fear Rion any more. He wasn't worth a moment of her time.

Rion had fooled her and used her. It was that simple. The words *bartered bride* sprang to mind...

'You and I were never friends, Rion,' she said bluntly. 'And I never needed your forgiveness. If anything it was the other way round. But, as you said, it was a long time ago and long forgotten.'

'Oh, come on, Selina.'

His hand reached around her waist and pulled her closer. She felt the heat of his body through the few inches of space separating them and her heart skipped a beat.

'I found you in bed with another man, not the

other way round as you tried to imply in the divorce.'

It was the arrogant drawl and the mockery that cooled her senses. 'I didn't have to try. Anyone knowing your reputation with women believed me. Whereas *you* leapt at the chance to name me an adulteress wife simply because a drunken boy passed out in the wrong bed,' Selina shot back flippantly, though she was battling to still her suddenly racing pulse.

'You know me so well, it seems, Selina,' Rion said, his lips twisting in a smile as his hand fell from her waist. He straightened up, and there was not a hint of amusement in the dark eyes that clashed with hers. They were as hard and cold as ice.

'My problem was I never knew you at all.' She shook her head. 'But it no longer matters,' she said, taking a step back. 'Now, I must check the kitchen.'

Rion's eyes narrowed on her flushed, determined face. That she had the nerve to try and defend the indefensible with a feeble excuse that a drunk had passed out in her bed was unbeliev-able, and fuelled his anger and determination to have her back in his bed.

With a shrug of his broad shoulders he moved to one side to let her pass. 'Oh, it matters, Selina. But I can wait.'

Wait? What for? Selina wondered. They had nothing to say to each other—never had, really. She had been an innocent, gullible teenager who had fallen madly in love with the first man who kissed her, and it had suited Rion to marry her at the time. She had been taken for a fool and discarded at the first opportunity he could find because he had got the company he wanted. It was that basic. And why was she wasting her time thinking about the past? She had moved on years ago, and in a day or two she could go back to her normal life, where her focus was really needed.

She walked past him, her head high, and made it to the kitchen. With a smile for Anna, busy arranging pastries on a tray, she took a bottle of water from the fridge. She picked up a glass from the bench and sat down at the table with a sigh of relief. She poured the sparkling water into the glass and, lifting it to her lips, drank most of it down in one go.

'You look like you needed that,' Anna said, and the compassion in the older woman's dark eyes restored Selina's mood a little.

'You are right, Anna—I did.' Selina sighed. 'I never expected the funeral service to be so long. I thought I was going to faint with the heat at the graveside.' It had nothing to do with the hateful Rion and her recent brush with him.

'Not surprising. It has been a stressful day for everyone. But hiding in here won't help.'

'I'm not hiding—simply taking a break from the guests. Most of whom I don't know anyway,' Selina said truthfully.

But she harboured no doubts that they all knew her, and knew the lurid stories about her. From illegitimate granddaughter to adulterous wife, she thought bitterly.

'One guest you know well: Orion Moralis. I'm sorry, it must have been a shock for you seeing him here. It never occurred to me he that would come to the funeral, because after you left he never spoke to your grandfather again. But I suppose it is the socially correct thing to do.'

'More likely good business,' Selina said dryly. 'And there is no need to apologize. I've spoken to Rion and we are friends—it is fine,' she lied.

'Thank goodness for that. Apparently his yacht arrived late last night. According to the gardener, who spoke to one of the crew this morning, they were heading to the Egyptian coast but diverted to here. It seems a lot of effort to attend the funeral of a man he had not seen in years. I was worried there might be something else, and I didn't want to see you hurt again.'

Anna knew the truth about their brief marriage. Selina had confided in Anna when she had so ignominiously been sent back to her grandfather, and Anna believed Selina's version of events.

'There is no fear of that happening,' Selina said, rising to her feet. 'Now the funeral is over and everything is settled I will be leaving tomorrow morning. I have a flight booked back to England tomorrow night, so I can spend a week with Aunt Peggy before returning to work. I promise, Anna, you have nothing to worry about. You can carry on as usual, looking after the villa until you want to retire. I know my grandfather will have taken care of you.' She knew this to be true, as her grandfather had told her so before he died. 'Now I'd better get back to the guests. Hopefully they will start leaving soon.'

'Good idea. I'll tell my two girls to slow down with the refreshments—that usually works.' Anna grinned.

Straightening her shoulders, Selina walked back into the main living room that opened out onto a wide terrace that overlooked the bay and noted that a lot of the guests were outside.

She spotted Rion at once. He was taller than everyone else and standing with two men— probably discussing business. From the couple of social events he had taken her to in the past, she knew that was all he ever did.

As she watched she saw him turn as an older grey-haired man joined the group. The man said something and Rion threw back his head and laughed, his hair shimmering black as a raven's wing in the sun, his teeth shining brilliant white against his olive-toned skin.

A little curl of heat rippled through Selina's body—because whatever else Rion was, there was no denying he was breathtakingly attractive. She was disgusted with herself for still reacting to the man, and yet she could not look away. But she wished she had as suddenly Lydia appeared and reached up to kiss Rion on the cheek.

Selina stiffened. It was a timely reminder. How had she not noticed Lydia at the funeral? Or the older man whose arm Lydia now casually looped through hers—obviously her long-suffering husband.

Poor fool, Selina thought cynically, her blood turning to ice in her veins. In that moment Rion looked across at her. Coolly she held his gaze, saw the mocking amusement in his eyes as he raised his glass. A gesture of recognition or in invitation to join the group? She didn't know or care which, and she turned and walked back inside.

She'd been cured of Rion ages ago, and what she had just witnessed in the garden confirmed her immunity. She strolled across to where the owner of the village bar and some of the other locals stood, and joined their group.

An hour later, with the whirring of helicopter blades, the guests began to leave. Selina smiled and listened to fulsome speeches until her jaw ached, and soon there was only Mr Kadiekis and a few villagers, chatting with a relaxed Anna and her daughters.

'You still here, Rion?' she asked with a frown as her ex-husband stopped in front of her. But her pulse didn't so much as flicker. She had assumed he had gone—or to be honest *hoped* he had... 'I thought you would have left by now. The gardener said you interrupted your cruise for the funeral. Very noble, but don't let us delay you any longer,' she said bluntly.

Rion arched a brow as he leant a broad shoulder against the wall, effectively blocking her view of most of the room.

'Your concern is touching, Selina, but I am not in any hurry. Obviously you still have an affinity with gardeners because your information is correct—I *am* taking a break.'

If his crude crack about gardeners was meant to rile her he was wasting his time. She was totally immune to him.

'Take a tip from me, Rion—a funeral is not a great way to start a holiday. So feel free to leave as soon as you like,' she said facetiously.

Rion straightened, trying to ease the almost permanent ache in his groin, which he had acquired since seeing Selina on the beach last night, her gorgeous body clad in the sexy white bikini. For an instant a vivid memory filled his mind. She had stood before him once wearing plain white briefs and a white cotton bra, a picture of innocence, her skin flushed and as soft as silk beneath his fingers as he undressed her completely, here on this island. He felt some indefinable emotion flow through him. Regret?

No. He dismissed the thought that swirled in his mind. He did not do emotions. He just wanted Selina again, and he was determined to have her by friendly means or foul. He didn't care which, so long as she was his soon.

'I intend to,' he said. 'But as you appear to be free of any male companion at the moment, I thought as an old friend you might like to join me on my yacht for a while.' He lifted a finger and brushed a tendril of hair behind her ear. 'You are no longer a teenager, Selina. You have changed into a feisty and exquisitely beautiful woman. I like the new you,' he said huskily. 'And the attraction between us is still there. We could have fun. What do you say?'

Rion's searching gaze swept over the beautiful face turned up to his. In a perfect scenario Selina would say yes, but he half expected an angry no. Her face revealed nothing. She didn't so much as blink.

'Your grandfather's death must have been stressful for you. A couple of weeks cruising will help you unwind, and we can get reacquainted.'

Still no response. Slowly it dawned on Rion that Selina was not reacting as he'd expected—not reacting at all...

'It is a very kind offer, but I am not interested, thank you,' she said politely, her usually expressive eyes oddly opaque.

From the first time they'd met the sexual attraction between them had been instant, and when they'd met again today, after years apart, Rion had recognised the sensual awareness still there when he held Selina, had seen it in her expressive eyes... Yet now he sensed complete indifference—not a reaction he had ever experienced in the women he met—and his jaw clenched in anger and frustration.

How did Selina *do* that? He wanted to grab

her and shake her, but most of all he wanted to be buried deep inside her.

After he had spoken to Kadiekis about the e-mail he'd received he had known immediately that he could use the information to his advantage, so he gave up on friendly and resorted to foul. Any sense of guilt he might have felt for exploiting Selina's current situation for his own satisfaction was outweighed by what she had done in the past. *Nobody* got the better of him—in business or otherwise—and got away with it. Few dared to try, but his oh, so innocent little wife had—with a deviousness he had never suspected she possessed. Now it was his turn.

'Think about it, Selina, and maybe for your own good you will change your mind,' he suggested silkily.

Selina was going to be his again, and he would make her forget every man she had ever known and enjoy doing it—until he tired of her and threw her out for good...

His dark gaze was shuttered, and Selina heard the threat in his tone, but it did not bother her.

'Don't hold your breath,' she mocked. Rion meant nothing to her now and she turned to walk away, not interested in him or anything he had to say.

Before she could move Mr Kadiekis stopped her.

'Selina, dear—and Rion.' He nodded to him. 'Nice to see you two getting on so well. It will make everything so much easier.'

Make what easier? Selina wondered—and then she had no more time to wonder as the lawyer carried on talking.

'I don't want to rush you, Selina, but my helicopter will arrive in less than an hour. So if we go to your grandfather's study now I can explain his will and answer any queries you may have.'

'Yes, okay. I'll just go and get Anna,' Selina offered.

'No need—you can give her the relevant information later.'

Selina caught a flicker of unease in the lawyer's eyes before he took her arm. To her surprise he told Rion to follow them.

She heard Rion agree, but did not see the triumphant glance he shot her as Mr Kadiekis ushered her into the study.

CHAPTER THREE

MR KADIEKIS took the chair behind her grand-father's desk and Rion lowered his long length down on the battered hide sofa against the wall. Ignoring him, Selina took the straight-backed chair at the side of the desk and sat down, still puzzled as to why Rion had been invited and not Anna.

Half an hour later Selina was no longer puzzled. She was incandescent with rage. Her grand-father had lied to her again…

After decades of faithful service from Anna and her husband, who had died in the same accident as his own son, Mark Stakis had not mentioned his housekeeper in his will at all—not even a token sum. Anna would be so hurt if she knew, and immediately Selina decided Anna was never going to find out what an ungrateful old rogue Mark Stakis had been. Not for the sake of his reputation, but for Anna's peace of mind. She was determined to do whatever it took to make sure Anna got the security she had so obviously earned and deserved.

Selina had inherited everything—not something she had expected or wanted. Maybe her grandfather had known her well enough to know she would take care of Anna, but it did not alter the fact he had lied to her.

As for her inheritance—in reality it was a double-edged sword. Mark Stakis had few assets left, and any money was tied up in such a way as to cost Selina dear. According to Mr Kadiekis in the past few years her grandfather had taken to gambling online in a big way. Shares, poker and sports—he would bet on anything, saying it was the only pleasure he had left. Consequently the house in Athens had been sold long since, and this villa was mortgaged to the hilt. His only income had been the twice yearly dividend from his Moralis shares which, as the lawyer pointed out, was luckily controlled by Orion Moralis!

Luckily... Selina certainly did not *feel* lucky. She could not believe it. But she had caught the gleam of triumph in Rion's dark, mocking eyes and she knew the lawyer was correct. She had to deal with the situation.

Battling to control her rage, she mentally reviewed the options open to her—precious few... Calmly she suggested Rion buy back the shares, thus enabling her to take care of Anna. The housekeeper need never know. But Rion refused, saying he preferred to 'discuss it later.'

Mr Kadiekis said he was confident they would work something out and he would abide by what they decided, but he had his helicopter to catch, and ended the meeting by telling Rion to get in touch with him when they had reached an agreement. It enraged Selina still further...

Convinced all Greek males had to be chauvinists from birth, Selina escorted the lawyer out of the villa, her mind whirling as fast as the blades on the helicopter waiting on the lawn. Stunned at what she had learnt, she watched Mr Kadiekis board and the machine take off before turning to go back inside.

Rion was leaning casually against the door frame, watching her with heavy-lidded narrowed eyes, his thick lashes flicking against his high cheekbones.

'I think now it is time you and I had that discussion, Selina Taylor,' he mocked, using her full name as stated in the will.

The damned, awful, bloody will... Selina swore under her breath and tightened her lips, because she didn't trust herself to respond to the hateful man. Instead she tried to walk back inside—but she had only taken a step when Rion caught her upper arm and spun her back from the door, leading her around the far corner of the villa.

'Let go of me,' she snapped, her eyes spitting fury as she tried to twist free of his grasp. 'You knew about this, you bastard.'

'Harsh words, but calling me names won't help you, Selina. Only I can.' A cynical smile twisted across his face. 'You would do well to remember that.'

Selina stopped struggling. Much as she hated to admit it, she needed Rion's agreement. Stiffening her spine, she looked straight at him. 'You're right, of course. I'm sorry,' she apologised—though it choked her to do so. But antagonising the mighty Orion Moralis would get her nowhere.

'Apology accepted.'

'Magnanimous swine,' she murmured under her breath. In cool, measured tones in sharp contrast to her furiously beating heart she said, 'Put it down to shock. It is not every day a woman of twenty-four discovers she has a guardian.'

'Understandable,' he said with a shrug of his broad shoulders, and let go of her arm. 'I'm guessing you do not want Anna to hear us before we reach a satisfactory arrangement, so let's take a walk. The pavilion is not far, and it's private. I seem to remember it always was before,' he prompted, and strolled on, expecting her to follow him.

Silently fuming, Selina took a step and stumbled forward. It had nothing to do with his mention of the pavilion—a place where Rion had kissed her senseless and a lot more... Damn it! He was getting to her again. She vowed to act cool and controlled until she got him to agree with her and left.

Then Rion turned and looped an arm around her waist to steady her. She forgot her vow and tried to jerk free, but his strong arm tightened, holding her pressed firmly to his side.

'Behave, Selina,' he ordered. 'To convince Anna, we will have to present a united front, and fighting is not going to do it.'

He was right again, and reluctantly Selina walked beside him, acutely aware of Rion's towering presence as he continued to walk and talk.

'Most people would say you have nothing to worry about. Your grandfather has left you his five-percent share in the Moralis Corporation, which I can assure you brings a quite substantial income by any standards. The fact that Stakis sold the house in Athens and mortgaged the villa having lost all his money gambling I knew nothing about until today.'

Still simmering with anger at the unfairness of the situation—and other emotions she preferred not to recognise—Selina glanced up at his harshly handsome face. His expression was bland, giving nothing away, and yet still he exuded an aura of power and a sheer masculine sex appeal that was hard to ignore. But ignore it she did. Been there, done that and never again. She was immune…

This was purely business, she staunchly reminded herself. Not that anything about Rion—business or otherwise—was ever pure, she thought bitterly.

'Maybe you didn't know about his gambling, but you sure as hell knew he made his will the weekend of our engagement party and never changed it,' she flung at him as, with his arm clasped firmly around her, he ushered her down through the old olive grove to the pavilion. 'I'm not eighteen any more so don't take me for an idiot, Rion. You must have insisted on being in control of the shares for twelve years as part of the deal you made with my grandfather to marry me and take over his company.'

Rion tensed and stopped a few feet away from the trellised archway of the pavilion, his arm falling from Selina's waist and his hands curling into fists at his sides. How the hell had Selina heard about the deal his father and Stakis had arranged? Only three people had ever known, and his father would never have said anything. Rion certainly had not...

'Who told you that?' he demanded. It had to have been Stakis. He had never liked the man. He'd been a devious old devil—as he knew better than most—but to tell his own granddaughter that he had used her to seal a business deal was cruel...and not strictly true...

Finding she was free from Rion's confining hold Selina glared up at him. 'I didn't know before I married you, that's for sure, and who told me does not matter. The fact you don't deny it is enough,' she said flatly. 'But to convince my grandfather before we were even married to make you the sole trustee of any shares I might inherit until I reached thirty was genius—a great bit of business on your part,' she said scathingly. 'I can't believe the lawyer insists it is legal. We have been married and divorced, for heaven's sake! And where did Kadiekis get the idea you and I get on so well that it would be fine? He could have only got that from *you...*'

Rion's face was impassive, but she noted lines of strain around his firm mouth.

'Unless you want the world to see and hear you ranting, I suggest we go inside,' he said curtly, and placing a hand in the middle of her back, he urged her forward through the arch into the pavilion.

Selina stopped dead and glanced around, her breath catching in her throat. Nothing had changed: the same plump blue cushions—faded now—were stacked along the deep padded seat that doubled as a daybed against the back wall of the pavilion. The only other furniture was a wooden table with a dead pot plant on top. The pavilion had been built for the grandmother

Selina had never met. According to Anna, the poor woman had suffered from a weak heart and crippling arthritis in her later years. This had been her favourite view of the bay. She had died three years before her son and his family— a blessing, in a way...

Not a lucky place, and haunted by ghosts, Selina thought bitterly.

Rion left her where she stood and dropped down on the bench, discarding his jacket and tie. He needed time to assimilate the fact that Selina had found out about the marriage deal...

The irony was that a week after meeting Selina he would have done just about anything to get her into bed, he'd wanted her so badly...

When he finally had he'd been so out of control for the first time in his life he had had sex without protection. With the prospect of a pregnancy in the mix, as well as the business, he had asked her to marry him. Selina had been ecstatic, his father and Stakis had been delighted, and Rion had felt supremely confident that he had made the right decision all around. He would like a son and heir someday, and with the virgin Selina at least he would be sure he was the father.

Maybe her hearing about the marriage contract went some way to explaining why Selina had betrayed him with another man. She had been so naive when they'd married—so open in her avowals of love. After the divorce he had realised cynically she had simply been enamoured of her introduction to sex. But for all that, she had been a refreshing change from the women Rion had known before. She must have been hurt and disillusioned, learning that he'd married her as part of a business deal, and had got back at him in any way she could.

But betray him she had, and it was something he could never forget. Not once, but twice—first by leaping into bed with another man and then with the conditions of the divorce.

Now he just wanted her body—and he was wasting time.

Selina turned to lean against the archway and look out over the headland. The interior of the old pavilion held too many memories, and she had to focus and get out of here as quickly as she could.

'I am not going to rant—I simply want to get this untenable situation settled as soon as possible,' she finally responded, having heard the rustle of cushions as Rion sat down. She did not turn her head. 'My only concern is Anna and her family. As I said, you can buy back your shares and—'

'Enough, Selina,' Rion interrupted. 'Much as I admire your glorious long hair, I flatly refuse to talk to the back of your head. Come and sit down and we can discuss your problem as reasonable adults.'

Rion was her problem, Selina thought scathingly. Ignoring his compliment about her hair, she took a few deep breaths in an attempt to stay calm. Unfortunately she needed his agreement for Anna's sake, so slowly she turned to face him—and her breath caught in her throat at the sight of him.

He had taken off his jacket and removed his tie, opened the top few buttons of his shirt, revealing the strong column of his throat and the beginnings of black curling hair on his bronzed chest. With his long legs stretched out before him he looked totally at ease and as sexy as sin...

She stiffened, banishing the guilty blush that rose in her cheeks at the wayward thought. With a mighty effort of self-control she swiftly raised her gaze to his face. There was nothing easy in the dark eyes that met hers, she realised, but a cold predatory gleam that threatened her in some way. A flicker of fear trickled down her spine.

'I am not going to jump on you, Selina. It is safe to sit down. I seem to remember the last time we were here you were not wary but willing.'

He had sensed her fear. The damn man could read her mind.

Marshalling her thoughts, she picked her words carefully. 'I was an infatuated young fool,' she said slowly, realising that if she hoped to win Rion over to her way of thinking there was no point in arguing over trivia. Reluctantly she sat down, leaving as much space between them as the close confines of the pavilion allowed. 'But, just so we understand each other, age and experience have taught me caution. Now, can we get down to business?'

Underneath she was silently seething. As if she needed reminding that it was in this pavilion that Rion had made love to her for the first time and then asked her to marry him. She'd been hopelessly in love with Rion and of course she had said yes. Later she'd realised he had seduced her and married her for business reasons. And now she knew more than she'd ever wanted to know about the sex business, she thought grimly.

'You were never a fool, Selina—quite the opposite. Few if any people get the better of me, but you did,' he said, shooting her a dry glance. 'Yet sitting here I find this place brings back so many memories. I remember when we had sex for the first time. You gave yourself to me so sweetly, so eagerly, you blew my mind.'

The husky tone of his voice got to her and she could not look at him. Instead she stared straight ahead at the view of the bay. The sea was shimmering in the golden rays of the setting sun.

Gave herself so sweetly! Blew his mind! Once Selina had believed that with all her heart. Rion had kissed her and the world had ceased to exist. In between kisses the daybed had been opened and he had undressed her and encouraged her to do the same, and she had gazed in wonder at his magnificent naked body as he had laid her down on the bed and joined her. She had known she'd been born for this moment—this man. She had given herself rapturously, eagerly, totally mesmerised by him.

Six years ago she had been fathoms deep in love with Rion and utterly convinced he felt the same way about her. It had only been later— much later—that she'd realised she had been seduced by a master player, and the pain had been like a knife in her heart. For months after she'd asked herself how could she have been so stupid as to believe a handsome, wealthy business tycoon like Rion Moralis had married her for love.

After the wedding he had installed her in his

bachelor apartment and carried on with his life as usual—working sixteen-hour days, business trips abroad—while she had spent her days sightseeing and her evenings waiting for Rion to come back and take her to bed.

At first she had made dinner every night—until at Rion's suggestion she'd stopped, because he'd rarely known what time he would be back, and it had been simpler to have dinner delivered, which was what he had done before. In the nightmare week after they parted she had worked out that he had only taken her to a restaurant three times and twice to a party in the whole time they were married. He had probably spent more time with his other women than he ever had with her.

Then to be confronted by his lawyer and her grandfather and told Rion wanted a quick divorce on the grounds of *her* adultery had been the final straw.

Men, who needed them? Selina thought scathingly. She had a father who had paid *not* to know her and a grandfather and a husband who had used her for their own benefit.

It was anger and the injustice of it all that had finally saved her sanity. She had returned to England and told Beth the whole story, and to Beth's credit she hadn't said *I told you so.* Though on the day of Selina's wedding Beth had tried to warn her that it was all a bit quick. With hindsight she should have listened. Instead she had gone ahead, convinced all her dreams had come true.

It had turned into a nightmare, and at her friend's suggestion she had spoken to Beth's father—an international lawyer—and with his help had found the courage to hit back. It hadn't eased the ache in her heart but it had done wonders for her self-esteem…

Rion was so handsome, so physical, and so outside her experience. He had overwhelmed her and she had fallen headlong in love with him the night they'd met. He had called her a few days later and taken her out to dinner a couple of times. Then three weeks after they'd met

Rion had accepted her grandfather's invitation to spend the weekend at the villa and seduced her...

The rest was history... And the present was all she cared about.

'Cut out the ramble down memory lane, Rion, and let's get to the point,' Selina said curtly. She was *not* going to let him think he could seduce her with a few soft words. She wasn't that girl any more. The fact he had just said '*we had sex* for the first time'—not made love, as she had once naively imagined—simply confirmed her rock-bottom opinion of the man and defiantly she held his gaze.

The atmosphere between them simmered with sexual tension, and something in the depths of his black eyes made her temperature rise and her temper quickly follow suit. Swallowing hard, she regained control of her senses. Rion could spot any weakness a mile off and she would not give him the satisfaction of knowing he still affected her. Business was his thing, and now it was hers.

'Contrary to what you think, I don't want

anything for myself. But I do care about Anna and her daughters. They mean more to me than my grandfather ever did. Not content with setting me up to marry you, he actually lied on his deathbed—he said he had taken care of Anna.' She shook her head in disgust. 'Naturally Anna must stay at the villa, and as you are my trustee for the next few years I need to know the share dividends will cover the mortgage, enable me to give Anna a decent sum of money *and* pay her salary for as long as she wants to work. Preferably you'll buy your shares back, which hopefully will give me enough to pay off all the debts and take care of Anna. Then I never need see you again. Make up your mind fast. I know how valuable your time is.' She could not resist the facetious dig. 'Plus I have a flight booked from Athens tomorrow evening, and I want everything settled before I leave.'

Abruptly straightening up, Rion turned sideways and let his gaze rest on Selina. Conflicting emotions were battling within him and he was not happy with that. She was really exquisite, with her long red-gold hair framing her face and falling around her slender shoulders, the soft swell of her breasts beneath the silk of her dress and her long legs neatly crossed at her ankles. There was a reserve about her, but also an innate sensuality that nothing could disguise, and he could feel the rush of blood to his groin…the tightening of arousal. Her small chin was tilted at a determined angle and her amber eyes stared coldly at him.

He frowned. The innocence he had admired when they'd met had well and truly gone, he realised with a tinge of regret but no surprise. Selina had the nerve to say she never wanted to see him again, but *he* was the injured party, he reminded himself. He had caught her in bed with another man and there must have been many more since then…

Rion let his anger at her betrayal fill his mind and easily regained control of his body. He would take Selina, enjoy her, then cut her out of his life for ever… But first he was curious to know why she needed money.

'Anna is not my concern,' Rion finally responded. 'Though commendably you have made her yours. What I find odd is why *you* need money so quickly. I gave you a generous settlement for a brief nine weeks of marriage...I'd be interested to know what you have been doing since the divorce to spend it all.'

He casually slipped his arm along the back of the seat and let his hand rest on her shoulder. He felt the slight quiver in her slender frame.

'As you know I'm a businessman, and I don't throw good money after bad.' He watched her long lashes lower, masking her expressive eyes, and knew she was not as unaffected as she pretended. He waited...

Selina was no longer cool. She wanted to shrug Rion's hand off her shoulder, but the past few years had taught her to show no weakness where men were concerned, and bluntly she told him the truth.

'I went to university, as originally planned. Aunt Peggy called to tell me I had passed my exams the week before we married. I was offered a place at university. She suggested I accept and then talk it over with you later. I agreed simply to keep her happy,' she said honestly. 'I mentioned it to you the same night, but you barely listened in between taking calls and working on your laptop as usual…' She shot Rion a scathing glance. 'Anyway, when I returned to England at the end of September luckily I was in time to take up my place at university. Three years later I got my degree, and since then I have travelled the world as a translator. Mandarin and Arabic are very popular and always in demand. I make a good living. I gave the bulk of my settlement to a children's charity.'

Selina did shrug her shoulder now, hoping to dislodge the disturbing warmth of Rion's hand from her skin, but it didn't happen.

Orion Moralis—a highly successful man of the world—was for an instant struck dumb. He'd had no idea Selina had accepted a place at university. He had naturally assumed that when she'd agreed to marry him she had given up the idea of further study. Had he really been so arrogant, so insensitive, he barely listened to her?

Yes, he had, he realised. Her willing body in his bed had been enough for him and he had never given much thought to anything else. Work had been his main priority at the time.

For a moment he was slightly ashamed. Then he remembered the divorce…and exactly how clever Selina was. He was not surprised she'd got her degree—but as for the rest…

He glanced down at her, his dark eyes narrowing as they met cool amber and then roamed over the beautiful face, the sultry pink lips that invited a kiss. 'Very noble of you,' Rion offered, but the cynic in him found it hard to believe she'd given that much money to charity.

She was a sophisticated lady, so she had travelled the world and enjoyed the high life till the money ran out, probably. But he had never met a more sensual woman. He only had to look at Selina even now to be turned on, and he knew he was not alone among the male population. Hell! Seeing a face and body like Selina's, a host of men would queue up to employ her even if she spoke gibberish. The dress she wore was designer label, as were the shoes. He knew because he had bought a few in his time, and it was more than likely some man had provided them for *her*... Not that it mattered to him—in fact, it made it easier.

'In that case, Selina, I am certain we can make a deal.'

CHAPTER FOUR

Selina glanced up at Rion. His statement was music to her ears.

'You are…? We can?' she exclaimed with a relieved smile. 'Thank heaven for that. I'll go and tell Anna.' She made to rise but Rion's arm slid from the bench down her back, his hand gripping her side.

'Not so fast, Selina. You have not heard what I am offering.'

Suddenly Selina was acutely aware of how close they were. Never mind worrying about Rion's touch on her shoulder—she knew she was in much deeper trouble. The pressure of his long-fingered hand against her ribcage was perilously close to the underside of her breast. He moved slightly, his taut thigh pressing against her leg, and to Selina's dismay she could feel an old familiar heat flooding through her veins.

How had that happened?

'In any successful deal both parties have to be satisfied, you would agree?' Rion queried, his dark eyes boring down into hers.

She would have had to be blind not to notice a different question in the black depths. Selina tensed as her stomach lurched, and she fought to break free from the hypnotic power of his intent gaze.

'Yes.' She nodded her head to break eye contact. An inner voice of reason was telling her she must get this conversation over with as quickly as possible, while her body was telling a different story. Her immunity to Rion was suddenly taking a stomach-churning nosedive.

'Good. I'm quite happy to cancel the trust and buy back the shares you hold at their present value.' Rion mentioned a sum of money that made Selina gasp. 'You will easily have enough to take care of Anna and do whatever else you want to do.'

'That's very generous of you. I'll—'

'I haven't finished,' Rion cut in, his free hand

sweeping back the long length of her hair from one shoulder to curve around the nape of her neck. A thumb seemingly idly stroked her throat, making each separate nerve end tingle and tauten in response. 'To satisfy *me,* Selina, I want you to join me on the yacht for the next two weeks—as my lover.'

Fighting against the sensual awareness that his close proximity aroused, Selina thought for a moment she had heard wrong...Rion *couldn't* have asked her to be his lover... Then she looked into his eyes and for a moment was transported back in time. The desire in the black depths was a potent reminder of what they had once shared.

Helplessly, she stared at him, her mind screaming that he was worthless, she hated him, even as her pulse accelerated like a rocket in shameful response to the promise of passion in his gaze, to the warmth of his hand curved around her neck.

Then he spoke, and as the import of his words sank in she snapped back to reality.

'Think of it as the honeymoon we never had, Selina, but without the marriage. No strings attached. I buy back the shares, you get the money, and no further contact between us—business or otherwise—will be necessary.'

Her eyes widened and she glared with rising anger at his handsome face. He was smiling complacently. How *dared* the arrogant devil assume he could walk back into her life and insult her by trying to blackmail her into his bed when he had so spectacularly thrown her out before? It was too incredible to believe! And to actually suggest calling the trip a honeymoon was so callous—the man had to have about as much sensitivity as a block of granite. But why was she surprised? she asked herself. She already knew that...

They had spent their wedding night on the Moralis yacht, cruising back to Athens. Rion had promised to take her on a dream honeymoon a week later but it had never happened...

Selina's lips moved but she could not get the words out, too furious to make a sound.

'If you really care about Anna you will agree. As you said yourself, Selina, you are no longer a teenager but an experienced woman of the world. You must have had quite a few lovers—some good, some not so good… But you already know we are compatible, and a trip on my yacht will be fun. At least you'll know what you are getting.'

A few lovers! Fun! The assumptions and the arrogant conceit of the man so enraged Selina she was almost apoplectic. Grasping his hand at her side, she determined to break free.

Rion had put totally the wrong interpretation on her silence. She opened her mouth to tell him exactly what she thought of his disgusting proposal, but before she could say a word his arm tightened around her ribcage like a band of iron. His thumb scraped over a nipple, the fine fabric of her dress no deterrent to the hardening peak. His mouth captured her parted lips in a seductive kiss, his tongue exploring the moist interior with a subtle eroticism that soon changed into a blazing statement of intent.

Stirred on different levels—excitement, anger—Selina knew she should resist. But it had been so long since she had been held kissed and caressed by a man…and the fact that it was Rion, her one and only lover, had a catastrophic effect on her self-control.

She trembled, and sensations she had repressed for years cascaded through her body overwhelming her defences. Involuntarily she reached for his broad shoulders and clung to him as the kiss she had thought to resist turned into a passionate seduction of all her senses, and she responded eagerly, matching his passion with her own.

His mouth left hers and she stared up into his dark eyes. She saw smouldering passion overlaid with a hint of male triumph, and the haze of desire slowly faded from her bemused mind. She lowered her head and let her hands fall to her sides. She was reeling with shock, mortified by the force of the emotions he had unleashed in her, and for the first time in years she blushed. She didn't dare look at him.

His hand twisted in the long length of her hair and tilted her head back so she had no choice but to face him. 'Ah, Selina, there is no need to blush.' He pressed a kiss to her brow and brushed her lips with his as his arm fell from her waist. Only his hand in her hair was keeping her captive. 'In fact I'm amazed you still *can* blush—and it is good to know the chemistry is as explosive as ever,' he murmured against her mouth. His lips trailed across her cheek, his breath warm on her ear. 'Trust me, you won't be disappointed.' And, lifting his head, he smiled into her eyes. 'Agreed, Selina?' Freeing her hair, he smoothed the curling tendrils over her shoulders

Furious with Rion, but even more furious with her helpless reaction to him, she wanted to slap the triumphant smile off his face. Okay, so he could turn her on with a kiss and a caress, but then Rion was the type of man who could probably turn on *any* woman from eighteen to eighty. He had certainly had plenty of practice, Selina reasoned.

But to insult her with his crack about blushing, and then in his arrogance ask her to trust him and think she would fall into his arms like a besotted idiot, ready to do his bidding... Well, he had another think coming...

He was in for a rude awakening.

She shoved him hard in the chest and leapt to her feet, fighting to control her breathing and her rage. She gathered her scattered thoughts before turning around to look down at him, lounging back against the bench, watching her with narrowed eyes.

'In your dreams, maybe—but not mine, Rion. I'm no longer the naive girl you married, and I don't have to agree with anything you say any more,' she told him scathingly. 'If I can't get the money for Anna it is not the end of the world. I *do* own the villa, and she can stay in it for the rest of her life. As for the mortgage—I can take care of it and her salary for six months. You may be the trustee of my inherited shares until I am thirty, but you can't refuse to pay me the dividends every six months—and if you try, I will take you to court. And we both know you would not want that.'

Selina was proud of her spirited response, even

if her heart was beating erratically, and she silently congratulated herself on her mature, reasoned reply. So, okay, she had slipped a dig in at the end—call it female vanity—but she saw no harm in reminding the superior swine that he had not always got his own way...

Rion, his mouth tightening, icily furious, looked at Selina, standing a few feet away, her lips swollen from his kiss, her face flushed, but with defiance in her glittering eyes and every line of her sexy body. That the deceitful witch had the audacity to threaten him a second time with court had ignited his temper all over again. Yet he had a sneaky admiration for her nerve. But she was right—there was nothing innocent about her any more, and he had heard more than enough... He stood up.

He had not thought he was a very vengeful man, and he had had no intention of going to Stakis's funeral. But when Mr Kadiekis had informed him he was still a trustee named in the will and his presence was needed at the reading, which was to take place straight after the funeral as Selina Taylor, the only beneficiary, planned to leave the next day, he had changed his mind.

Learning she had come back to claim her inheritance had reignited a bitter rage in Rion that he had buried for six years. He had never considered contacting Selina, but having her served up on a plate was a different matter. Then, when he'd seen her again last night— a stunningly beautiful woman, sexy as hell, frolicking in the sea and hardly the grief-stricken granddaughter—revenge had sounded better and better.

'You are either very brave or very stupid, Selina,' he offered. 'I let you get away with your slanderous lies last time because it suited me to get a quick divorce, but it won't work a second time.'

Rion stepped closer and saw her flinch.

'Sorry to disappoint you, but the Moralis Corporation is family-owned, as I'm sure your grandfather told you. I am the major shareholder, along with Helen and Iris, and you are the fourth and very minor last,' he said, his derisive tone a deliberate insult. 'I am in control and there will be no dividends unless I say so. But it was a nice try...' he drawled mockingly.

'You can't do that!' Selina exclaimed, stunned by his revelation, but watching Rion tower menacingly over her she had a horrible sinking feeling he could. 'I mean...'

'I can do what I want, and right now I want you. But my time is limited.' He tipped up her chin with one long finger, his dark eyes capturing hers. A shiver of fear snaked down her spine—but not enough to quell the lingering heat in her body aroused by his kiss. She shook her head and his finger fell away, but it wasn't much help to her. He was still too close.

'There is an American expression: three strikes and you're out. This afternoon I invited you as a friend to join me on my yacht for two weeks—you look tired, like you could use a break. Then I offered to make a deal that is acceptable to you. Now I am *telling* you: my yacht is leaving at midnight. Agree to come with me or you are out.'

'But...'

Wide-eyed and wary, Selina stared at him, her hands curling into fists at her sides, trying to hold herself together while her thoughts were in chaos. The fact that Rion thought she looked a wreck niggled, and didn't help her confidence. Blinking, she ran her financial status through her mind and realised there was no way she could personally keep Anna—she had other vital commitments...

'What will I tell Anna? I thought...'

What *had* she thought? That a man like Orion Moralis would agree out of the goodness of his heart? Hadn't she learnt years ago he did not have one? Maybe she *was* still naive—because it had never occurred to her that Rion would withhold the dividends.

'Agree and we will go and see Anna together. I will back whatever you want to tell her,' he said, extending a hand to her.

Selina glanced down at his strong, long-fingered hand. He had brought her to climax with those elegant fingers before... Her thighs flexed and, shocked, she stifled the memory, going hot and cold and hot again. Ignoring his hand, she glanced up, her gaze skating over his hard face. She saw the determination in his heavy-lidded eyes and knew he meant what he said. She went cold again.

'Why are you doing this?' Selina finally cleared her mind of the sexual fog Rion had induced and asked the question she should have asked in the beginning. 'You can have any woman you want—your list of lovers is legendary—so why me? We don't even *like* each other.'

'I like what I see, Selina darling,' he drawled, his gaze roaming over her in insolent appraisal. 'Very much so. And I want to see a lot more. You looked great in that tiny white bikini, but your naked body in my bed will look even better.'

The colour drained from Selina's face and her eyes widened in horror. Her instincts had been right last night—someone *had* been watching her.

'You were on the beach spying on me.' She

was angry and frightened but forced herself to stare coldly at Rion. 'That's disgusting.'

'No, quite the reverse—you looked beautiful and erotic playing in the sea, Selina.' His hand snaked out and caught her shoulder and she stiffened in rejection. 'So much so I decided to renew our acquaintance,' he mocked, his hard eyes narrowing on her pale face.

Selina shrugged, trying to dislodge his hold on her and at the same time hoping to convey her indifference to him—with no success.

'Well, you have. And flattered though I am,' she said with sarcastic bite, 'I can't just take off on holiday with you. I have commitments—work...'

Actually she was on holiday—she had a six-week break between jobs. She had planned to stay at home with Peggy for a couple of weeks, but she had already lost a week coming here, and then she had planned to help Beth with the charity for a month before her next assignment.

Even if she wanted to go with Rion—which she definitely did not—it was impossible.

'Let me enlighten you, Selina. You don't have a choice. To put it bluntly, it is payback time,' he drawled, with a silken menace that made her blood run cold.

She looked at him in disbelief. 'There is always a choice,' she said tightly.

'Not for you. Not this time. As far as I know you are the only woman to cheat on me with another man, which was bad enough, but to threaten me with a public fight over the divorce so I had to concede to your demands was worse. There is a saying: revenge is a dish best served cold. As by a quirk of fate, Stakis never changed his will. I decided it was time to take mine. Call it closure, if you like. As for your work commitments—if they *are* that—' he prompted, with a sardonic arch of an ebony brow '—cancel them and I'll pay you double what you lose in salary.'

Typical of Rion the businessman. Believing his wife had been unfaithful did not bother him half as much as not getting his own way in the divorce, and in that moment she hated him with a fury she could hardly contain.

Selina wanted to claw at his conceited, arrogant face and tell him to go to hell. But instead she counted to a hundred under her breath, fighting to maintain her self-control.

Tilting back her head, she swept her eyes over Rion, a scornful gleam in their golden depths. She knew exactly what he meant and was filled with revulsion—but sadly life had taught her not to be surprised. In a weird way it put things in perspective for her and finally cooled her temper, and she began to think seriously about his offer—or rather his ultimatum!

The life and death of Mark Stakis had put her in this position. Chance…fate…it didn't matter which. The question was, with her firmly held moral beliefs, could she walk away from Anna and her girls?

No, she would not be able to live with herself if she did…

Selina knew there was no other work on the island for Anna, and since the death of her husband she had been the only financial support for her daughters. Thea, the youngest, was joining her sister at college on the mainland in the autumn hoping to become a lawyer. There was no way Selina could destroy those young girls' dreams…which was what would happen if she walked away. She had spent the past few years trying to help children's much smaller dreams come true.

Rion was a filthy-rich powerful man, and what he wanted he got—money no object. And at the moment he wanted her… A cynical smile twisted her lips. The great Orion Moralis would be outraged if anyone dared suggest he paid for sex, and yet what he was suggesting was no different in her eyes.

She thought of her Aunt Peggy, whom she considered her family. Although Peggy had claimed her state pension two years ago naturally she still lived with Selina, and depended on her to a large extent. She would never dream of leaving Peggy to fend for herself, as her grandfather had done Anna. Then there was Beth and her husband, Trevor, and the charity they ran that needed Selina's regular financial support.

She made good money at her job, but it was not enough to cover any more commitments.

She stifled a despairing sigh. She needed the money from the shares she had supposedly inherited for Anna but she had to go through Rion to get it. Unfair, but then life wasn't always fair...

Selina thought of all the people she had met, some so very young, who had really suffered and sacrificed for their family—not for a couple of weeks but for years. Could she in all conscience do any less? she asked herself. How hard could it be to put up with Rion? He said he wanted her, but only for two weeks—no surprise there. He had the attention span of a flea where women were concerned. He scratched the itch and leapt on to the next...

She could 'lie back and think of England,' she supposed. A clichéd expression but probably true for many women...

Her decision made, she put her hand in Rion's. 'Agreed.' She shook his hand to seal the deal and swiftly pulled free. 'Now can I go and tell Anna the good news?'

'Yes, but first...' Rion wrapped an arm around her waist and pulled her hard against him. Cupping her chin between thumb and forefinger, he tipped her head back. 'Anna is an astute lady. You need to look the part.'

He was going to kiss her again, she knew and Selina splayed a hand on his chest to push him away, but with his shirt open her fingers made contact with satin-smooth flesh and her stomach churned.

'Yes, touch me, Selina.' His voice lowered to a husky growl and she felt the warmth of his skin beneath her palm as his mouth covered hers.

She tried to stay rigid in his arms, her mouth closed, and she did it for a few seconds. Then her lips quivered beneath the pressure of his as he circled them teasingly with his tongue. He bit her bottom lip, and involuntarily her mouth opened. He caught the tip of her tongue and sucked lightly before deepening the kiss, his tongue probing the interior of her mouth with a gentleness that sent shivers through her slender frame. His hand stroked down her neck and over her breast and finally her body betrayed her. She was eighteen again and eager, her resistance melting, and she kissed him back.

Rion felt the yielding softness of her body and broke the kiss. Her head was tipped back, her eyes closed and her lips parted, and he knew with little effort he could have her here and now.

Selina opened her eyes and Rion's mouth fastened over hers again. His hand moved to curve around her buttocks and involuntarily she pressed closer, felt the hard length of his arousal against her belly. His other hand cupped her breast, his long fingers teasing the burgeoning nipple through the silken fabric. The deep, searing kiss and the caress, the heat of his hard body, the scent of him—all so achingly familiar, and in seconds she was drowning in a sea of delight.

Rion heard her whimpering cry and felt her small hand stroke beneath his shirt. Stifling a groan, he knew he had to stop now or he wouldn't be able to, and he eased away, linking his hands behind her back.

'Ah, Selina.' He looked into her passion-hazed eyes. 'I think that is enough. Anna will have no trouble believing we are reconciled now.'

Enough? Reconciled? Selina came down to earth like a spent balloon, all the air knocked out of her, humiliatingly aware of how easily she had succumbed to Rion's brand of lovemaking. No, not love…just sex, she reminded herself. Something she must never forget again. Her body might be weak and hot but her heart would forever remain a block of ice where Rion was concerned.

'What do you mean, reconciled?' she asked, and took a step back. His arms fell from her waist and she glanced up at him, noting the dull flush on his high cheekbones and realising he was nowhere near as cool as he acted—which was some slight consolation.

'How else are you going to explain to Anna you are leaving with me tonight?'

'Well, I am sure as hell not going to tell her we are *reconciled*. Anna is not an idiot—she would never believe that,' she shot back, her mind spinning, searching for an answer. 'I told her earlier I was fine with you being here. She was worried you might be up to something, as you hadn't spoken to my grandfather in years.' Thinking on her feet, she added, 'I was due to leave tomorrow morning, but I have not booked a boat to the mainland yet. If I tell Anna you have offered to take me back to the mainland earlier, so I will have time to call on Mr Kadiekis to sign some legal documents and speed up the processing of the will before I fly out tomorrow night, I think she would quite easily believe me.'

'My, my, Selina!' Rion grinned. 'So quick-thinking and so devious. You have certainly matured. But I agree.' And, looping an arm around her shoulder, he led her out of the pavilion and back towards the house.

She made no attempt to break free.

Selina's mind was filling with the enormity of what she had agreed to with every step she took.

'You'd better decide quickly exactly what you are going to give Anna before we reach the house, Selina. Anna is not going to be convinced she is mentioned in the will if you are indecisive.'

Rion's businesslike comment was a timely reminder of why she had agreed with him—why she was strolling through the orchard with his arm around her—and it hardened her resolve to do the right thing by Anna.

'Anna can have the villa. I doubt I'll ever be back,' she said with a hint of bitterness. At the same time she wondered how she would explain to Beth she was going to be delayed because she was going on a two-week holiday with her ex-husband...

'Not a good idea. Anna would find it very hard to believe Stakis left her the house—and even if she did how could she possibly afford the upkeep of the place?' Rion pointed out. 'She would have to sell it, and the legal documentation would reveal you had owned it before you gave it to her, which would defeat your purpose of keeping Anna in the dark about the true contents of the will.'

'Oh,' she said, and it did not help realizing Rion was right.

'As I see it, you can give Anna a lump sum—say fifty thousand or, being generous, a hundred thousand—which you will easily be able to afford. As a local islander Anna will be able to get a house in the village for that. You keep the villa, and keep on employing Anna for as long as she wants to work. You can visit whenever you like, and rent it out as a holiday let the rest of the time. That way the villa will still be an asset for you. One day you might marry again, have children and want to live here—after all, you are half Greek.'

'I'm not in the least Greek, I will never marry again and I have no intention of having a child. There are enough in the world already that need looking after,' Selina said, finding her voice. 'As for Anna—you are right. I'll tell her she was left a hundred thousand.' She glanced up at Rion and saw he was frowning—strange when she had agreed with him! 'I need to make a few phone calls before I leave.'

She never lied, but now she was going to have to—three times in one day, she thought help-lessly. Selina knew Beth would readily accept she had decided to take a holiday and booked a cruise around the Mediterranean, and would be happy for her. Beth was always telling her she worked too hard and should take a break and relax. If she told Beth the truth she would be outraged and beg her not to go with Rion. She knew what a wreck Selina had been after her ill-fated marriage. There was no reason to upset Beth unnecessarily, and the charity needed every penny it could get…

CHAPTER FIVE

ALMOST midnight—the witching hour, Selina thought fancifully as she stood on the deck, her hands gripping the ship's rail as the luxury yacht slid smoothly out of the harbour of Letos. Thankfully it was a newer model than the one on which she had spent her ill-fated wedding night.

She was still stunned at how easily Rion had charmed Anna. He'd told her she had inherited a hundred thousand euros in the will, Selina had added that she wanted to continue to employ Anna to take care of the villa for as long as she wanted to work, and Anna had been so happy it was not surprising she'd believed everything Selina had said. She had accepted her story that it made sense to return to Athens with Rion so she would be there by the morning and have time to see Mr Kadiekis before flying out in the evening. So much so Anna had actually helped Selina to pack…

As soon as they'd come on board Rion had introduced her to the only other guest—Dimitri, a shaven-headed, fit-looking man in his fifties— telling her he would look after her for a while as Rion had to join the captain on the bridge and see the yacht safely out of harbour.

Dimitri had taken her bags and shown Selina to her cabin. He had explained how the computerised system worked and told her if she wanted anything to call. Then he'd told her Rion had the master cabin next door.

At least she had her own cabin, Selina thought with a sigh of relief. But even so, after unpacking her clothes and taking a quick shower, she had slipped on an old sweatsuit—enough to turn off any man, she thought. But five minutes later, unable to stand the confines of the cabin with its bed—a reminder of why she was there—she'd slipped on a pair of flip-flops and escaped to the deck.

But there was no escape for her, Selina realised. She must have been mad to agree to Rion's demand. She was never going to be able to do it… He was expecting an experienced lover—he had said as much—and she was the opposite. She had been celibate since their divorce. True, she had dated a few men, shared a kiss, but had never been tempted into a sexual relationship. She had seen more than enough of what it did to people and wasn't interested.

Rion descended the stairs to the main deck and stopped, drawing his black brows together in a frown. Selina was leaning over the rail, and even from this distance he could sense the tension in her. She did not want to be here, he knew, and felt a slight twitch of conscience. But she looked so gorgeous, with her long hair tied up in a ponytail dancing around in the sea breeze.

He noted she had changed the elegant dress for a baggy blue sweatshirt and pants, probably meant to put him off. But they were doing just the opposite. He felt his whole body respond and put his conscience aside. He had no need to feel guilty. Selina was getting what she wanted, like most women—money—and he was confident enough in his masculinity to know he could keep her satisfied and happy in his bed.

Selina smothered a cry of surprise as two strong arms folded around her waist. Lost in thought, she had not heard Rion approach. Letting go of the rail, she clasped his forearms, but the feel of his firm, warm skin against her palm made her catch her breath. The memory of another night and a different yacht, but with the same man doing exactly what he was doing now, flashed through her mind. And the memory of her avid response.

Not surprising, really, as after the first time they had made love Rion had never made love to her again, saying he wanted to wait and make the wedding night special. More likely he'd had some other woman—probably Chloe—warming his bed, she had realised later.

Stiffening, Selina turned her head to cast him

a sidelong glance. 'You surprised me. I thought you were with the captain.'

'I was, but you looked so alone.' His dark head bent and he nuzzled the back of her neck, her earlobe. 'I decided to keep you company.'

'There is no need,' Selina said, trying to hang on to her self-control, which was becoming harder to do by the second with the warmth of his breath against her ear and the slight spicy scent of his cologne. It was hard to suppress the old familiar feelings and the memories she had thought long forgotten.

'Trust me—there is,' he said huskily, nibbling her neck and then sucking the tiny pulse that beat there as his hand snaked up beneath her sweater to cup her breast. Kneading gently, his long fingers slid teasingly over the swelling peaks in a caress that made her shudder from head to toe.

Selina gasped, her heart pounding. Why had she thought a scruffy old sweatsuit was enough to deter Rion? And she wasn't wearing anything underneath, she thought helplessly. She tried to wriggle free from his hold—a bad mistake!

He pressed her back against his great body and she let her hands fall to her sides—and was immediately made aware of the strength of his masculine arousal against her buttocks.

'Feel what you do to me?' Rion rasped against the hollow of her throat, kissing and licking her tender skin.

'Let me go,' she got out shakily, her overheated body combining with the feeling of being completely surrounded by Rion making her head whirl. She grasped his arm at her waist, trying to prise herself free, but as she did so he rolled her aching nipples between his index finger and thumb, sending shafts of aching pleasure from her breasts to her loins, while his sensuous mouth lingered on the pulse that beat wildly in her throat, making her tremble, making her weak...

She raised her hands again, but with a will of their own her fingers seemed to glide up over his forearms, his muscular biceps.

'Don't...' she murmured desperately. 'Someone will see.' A low moan escaped her as the hand at her waist slipped beneath her sweatpants to splay across her bare stomach and finally to cup the delta of her thighs, while his other hand continued the delicious torment of her breasts.

'No one can see except perhaps the fishes,' Rion rasped. 'Relax and enjoy.'

'No...' she moaned. But against her will she was caught up in the wild, sensual hunger that rose from deep inside her as the past and the present collided in her mind. Her head fell back against his chest, her neck arching as he eased her legs slightly apart. His long, skilful fingers traced the delicate folds guarding her feminine core, searching the hot, damp centre with his fingertips, the pad of his thumb finding and stroking the tiny point of sensitive nerves to swollen pulsing pleasure... She was on fire, every nerve end taut with need...

'You like that, Selina. You want more,' he breathed against her ear, and nibbled on the tender lobe. 'You only have to ask,' he rasped.

She was trembling with need and yet a note of discord at his words pierced the sensual haze that was her brain. A flash from the harbour lighthouse spun across the water, dazzling her eyes and reminding her where she was.

'No, Rion.' She breathed his name and grasped his wrist, digging her fingers into his skin as much to quell her own desire as his intention.

Rion wasn't sure how it had happened so fast, but Selina had responded to everything he'd done to arouse her, and aroused him so much he was desperate to be inside her. And yet she had the strength of will to stop him. The girl he had married would never have done so—but the Selina of today was a much stronger character.

He knew with his superior strength and skill he could easily persuade her differently, but he was reluctant to do so. Maybe he had been crass to demand she ask him. But he had never known a woman so responsive, and he was not going to let her slip back into denial.

Sliding his arm around her, he turned her to face him. 'You're right, Selina, the cabin would be better.' And he stroked a hand up her back, holding her close, aware of the erratic beat of her heart. 'But no more games. We both know what we want.'

He dipped his head and kissed her long and deep, until he felt her relax against him, her slender arms sliding around his neck. Raising his head he smiled into her eyes.

'Bedtime, Selina,' he said, and swept her off her feet.

Aching with frustration, and dazed by his kiss, Selina clung to Rion's broad shoulders as he carried her through to his cabin and laid her down on a huge bed. She was intensely conscious of him—his dark chiselled features, the unfathomable depths of his eyes—and she wasn't capable of resisting or uttering so much as a word as he reached for her and deftly removed the baggy suit.

What was the point of resisting anyway? Even if she could—which she very much doubted. It was too late for that. They were at sea, and so were her emotions… The result was inevitable, because she had made a deal and she must honour it. An impish devil whispered in her mind: *So why not enjoy the experience?* No other man had ever made her feel the way Rion did and probably never would!

He'd said he wanted her naked in his bed and here she was. He had seen her naked dozens of times—well, maybe not. She had been a bit of a prude about walking around naked, unlike Rion who had often teased her about it. But now she was naked, exposed, and Selina had a moment of panic, glancing warily up at Rion looking down at her.

She saw the hunger and the dark desire in his eyes, and her heart missed a beat and another, as he stripped off his shirt, revealing his broad muscular chest with its sprinkling of black hair arrowing down his stomach. Then he took off his pants, and she swallowed hard as his magnificent bronzed body in all its masculine beauty was revealed to her no longer wary but wondering eyes. He was incredible. The strength and the power of his erection made her gasp and desire kicked in her belly, her body throbbing in hungry recognition.

Suddenly she felt totally inadequate. He was expecting an experienced lover. Weakly she asked, 'What do you want me to do?'

Rion stilled, hearing the catch in Selina's voice. His dark eyes sought hers and he saw the shadows in their amber depths. He didn't want her thinking she had to do whatever he said, he realised, even though he had given her little choice but to come with him.

His avid gaze roamed over her incredible naked body.

Selina was perfect—quite perfect: her glorious hair trailed across the pillow, her superb breasts and straining nipples, the flat stomach, the soft strawberry-blonde curls at the apex of her thighs, the long legs...

Rion wanted her badly—but he wanted her warm and willing. Lying down beside her, he raised himself up on one elbow and looked into her wide and wary golden green-flecked eyes. 'Just be the beautiful, sexy woman I know you are, Selina…' He brushed her lips with his. 'Let me do the rest.'

The strange thing was that it seemed the most natural thing in the world to be like this with him, Selina thought, but said nothing. The flush of desire burned her skin as he smoothed a hand along her shoulder.

She trembled as his lean hands shaped her waist, her thighs, and then moved back to let his fingers drift over her breasts, grazing the tight peaks.

He bent his head and kissed her with a gentleness, an aching warmth that surprised her, and she was seduced all over again by his tenderness. Her lips parted to taste him with her tongue, her hands moving of their own volition up his chest.

'Oh, yes…' Rion groaned against her mouth as she touched him, and he kissed her again with a demanding, possessive passion that sent electric sensations arcing through her, tightening her body, driving her wild.

His hand stroked down her belly, his long fingers playing with the soft curls at the juncture of her thighs before moving between the velvet lips, the tips teasing and stoking the fire in Selina's blood to fever-pitch.

Selina's hand clenched on his shoulder as arrows of liquid heat shot to her damp, pulsing core. She raked a hand through his dark hair and shuddered, wanting him...all of him...with a white-hot wanton passion. Her other hand reached for the velvet-and-steel length of him, her slender fingers barely closing around the thickened strength of him, moving, exploring.

Rion groaned, ready to explode. Fighting for control, he pulled her hand away and, dipping his head, captured a pouting nipple in his mouth while his long fingers explored the hot wet centre of her with delicate strokes.

Selina's eyes closed, her face taut with pleasure at his hungry suckling, the insistent harder rhythm of his fingers. She felt her muscles clench, her body lifting, trembling on the brink, then convulsing in shuddering release as Rion lifted her and, with one powerful thrust, filled her.

'Rion...please!' she cried, not sure she could take any more.

But she was wrong, and she was flung into a maelstrom of sensations that went on and on as his hard length stretched her and thrust deeper and faster, until with an answering cry Rion's great body shuddered, filling her with his very essence.

Rion rolled onto his back, weak with release but still with enough strength to take Selina with him, so she lay cradled across his heaving chest. He was shocked. He had never come so fast or so fiercely before—ever... Not even when they were married. Then he had been gentle with Selina, thinking to lead her slowly down the sexual highway.

Rion raised his hand to brush her silken hair back from her face, and found himself huskily apologising. 'Sorry I was a little quick, but it has been a while.'

Selina shifted against him, one slender leg brushing over his groin. Amazingly he felt himself stir again as she lifted her head and glanced up at him. 'You were fine,' she murmured, a dazed look in her gorgeous eyes, and let her head fell back on his chest.

'I'll make it better next time,' he said, and felt her body relax.

Next time, Selina thought—then stopped thinking and closed her eyes.

Rion held her close and stroked his hand gently over her head, let the silken strands of her hair slide seductively through his fingers. He brushed his lips across her brow and realised she was asleep. Next time was not going to be as soon as he had hoped, he thought, a rueful smile twisting his lips. But with the warmth and the weight of her body over his chest, the feminine scent of her filling his nostrils, he didn't really mind. He could wait...

Selina was his for the next couple of weeks— and, given her response, longer if he so chose, Rion thought with a sense of masculine satisfaction. He relaxed.

Then it hit him what he had done—or to be precise what he had *not* done...

Damn it to hell! he cursed. Only twice in his life had he forgotten, and both times with the same woman... His sense of satisfaction vanished like smoke in the wind.

'Selina—Selina!' He slid his hand from her head to her waist, to tip her onto the bed.

Snuggled against a hard, warm body Selina let her eyes flutter open. Someone was calling her name. For a moment she was totally disorientated—then suddenly she was lying flat on her back.

'What?' she muttered, and her eyes opened wide at the sight of Rion sitting up, his upper torso turned towards her. 'Is it morning?' she asked, though it wasn't daylight, she realised, but moonlight that illuminated Rion's bare chest and face.

Then it all came back to her. She was in Rion's bed and they had made love. Suddenly she was conscious of her own naked state and felt a slow tide of warmth spread through her body—not so much a blush, more an involuntary sensual response to the man looking down at her. But by

the thunderous expression on Rion's hard face
he was having no such reaction.

'I did not use any protection, Selina. I need to
know: Are you on the Pill?' he demanded

'You woke me up to ask that?' The warmth
seeped away and, sitting up, she reached for the
edge of the coverlet and pulled it over her chest.

'Yes, it is vital. I have no intention of being
trapped into becoming a father and paying for
it the rest of my life. I *never* forget to use a
condom, and I can assure you I am perfectly
healthy. I have regular check-ups—can you say
the same?'

Selina had heard some insults in her twenty-
four years, but Rion's took the cake! How like a
man. He didn't want to be trapped—no thought
for the woman who would have to carry the child
for nine months and look after it for the rest of
her life. All Rion was worried about was the
money it might cost him…

What a charmer. But then why was she surprised?

She considered stringing him along. Letting

Rion sweat for a few weeks would serve the arrogant devil right. But then that would involve her keeping in touch with him, and she didn't want that...did she?

'Lucky for you I *am* on the Pill.' Ironically, when she had returned to England after Rion had thrown her out she had consulted her GP about her cramps and he had put her on the Pill. 'And I had a check-up four months ago.' Which she had—but not for the reason he thought. 'I have not had a lover since. Can you say the same?' She repeated his own question with a cynical arched brow in his direction and then, swinging her legs off the bed she stood up, ignoring Rion.

'Good,' Rion said, and he felt good. Of *course* Selina was on the Pill—she was an intelligent, sexually active woman who took care of herself. It made perfect sense. 'And to answer your question yes, I *can* say the same. It seems we have both had a barren spell.' He chuckled, and looked at her shapely naked body as she bent down to pick up her sweatpants from the floor with her back towards him.

Suddenly Rion didn't feel so much fine as hungry. He was hardening again at the sight of her peachy bum slowly disappearing beneath the blue pants. He rolled off the bed and in one lithe movement reached for her arm and spun her around to face him.

'Why bother dressing? We have the night ahead of us and the best is yet to come,' he drawled, supremely confident of his virile prowess.

Selina's eyes widened on his as she saw rekindled passion in the deep black pupils, sensual invitation... Hastily she lowered her gaze, refusing to be tempted. But looking at him standing in front of her stark naked was no help. His big body gleamed in the moonlight and incredibly she saw he was aroused again. She felt a renewed flicker of desire flare inside her.

She stiffened and doused the flame. 'I'm going to bed. Dimitri gave me the cabin next door, and I prefer to sleep on my own,' she clipped.

Rion recognised her defiant stance and was infuriated as well as frustrated. 'Reneging on our agreement already, Selina? You are here as my lover, remember?' he told her bluntly.

His dark eyes flicked over her face, over the wild tangle of hair falling to her shoulders, the proud thrust of her full firm breasts, the rosy nipples still swollen from his mouth. Her slender arms were by her sides and her hands clenched into fists.

'Playing games will get you nowhere. You sleep in my bed unless I say otherwise.' Rion didn't know why he was insisting. He preferred sleeping alone. He had never spent a whole night with a woman in years—not since Selina...

Selina's shoulders slumped. 'Okay,' she said. He was so damn arrogant, and she was too exhausted to argue with him. There was no point anyway. Rion would do what he liked—he always did. In his business life and his private life. With a skill and cunning that rarely failed. She meant nothing to him other than a female to warm his bed for two weeks. She had to remember that.

Turning, she walked around the foot of the

bed and climbed in, pulling the coverlet up to her neck.

Just like that she had given in, and Rion was left standing like a lemon, watching her pull the cover over her body. He didn't know whether he felt pleased or angry. What was it about Selina that managed to confuse him so easily? Whatever it was, the bed beckoned, and he lay down beside her and drew her unresisting body into his arms.

'A kiss goodnight?' he drawled softly, lowering his dark head.

Selina glanced up into his handsome face, saw the sensuous intent in his black eyes. She could not help it. A wide yawn escaped her.

As a passion killer it was classic…

Rion's lips twitched in a wry smile. She was so beautiful, so very feminine—and so very tired, he realised belatedly. A pang of guilt stabbed at him, but though he had no doubt he could persuade her, he wasn't a selfish enough lover to try.

While Selina had been making calls to rearrange her work schedule Anna had told him that when the doctor had said Mark Stakis only had days left, not knowing who to call, she had rung Selina. Without hesitation Selina had dropped everything to come straight to Greece. She had sat at her grandfather's bedside for two days, only taking the occasional nap, until he died, and then she had arranged the funeral—contacting all the necessary people and holding up marvellously all day as a perfect hostess. Then Anna had asked him to make sure Selina caught her flight all right—because she really needed a rest.

Avoiding her lips, he pressed a kiss on her forehead. 'You're tired. Go to sleep.'

Selina needed no encouragement, and with a deep sigh she was asleep in seconds.

It took Rion a lot longer as Selina twisted restlessly in her sleep, ending up with a slender arm slanting down over his body, her hand splayed on his belly, her head resting on his chest and her firm breasts pressed against his side. Her steady breathing teased the hairs on his chest, and if her hand moved a fraction of an inch he would no longer be responsible for his actions.

CHAPTER SIX

Rion opened his eyes instantly, aware Selina had moved. He lay still, the heavy beat of his heart thudding against her breast and the deep rise and fall of his breathing stirring her hair. Her head was still on his chest, and the hand he had been wary of earlier was resting on his shoulder. It was the leg she had slid between his thighs that had aroused him from sleep—in more ways than one… Yet she seemed to be sleeping like a baby while he was hard and aching.

He ran a finger lightly up her spine, his other hand stroking gently down to her pert rear. She was warm and shapely, her skin as soft as silk beneath his hand and there was only so much frustration a man could stand, he decided. But before he could make a move, amazingly he felt her lush mouth kiss his chest, her hot little tongue licking a nipple to pebble-like hardness, her slender hand on his shoulder inching up his neck.

In their brief marriage she had flung her arms around him and kissed him enthusiastically when he'd returned home and when he'd made love to her she'd been amazingly responsive, yet rather shy, but she had never once initiated sex. Now...

Rion stifled a groan and waited in sensual anticipation of what she would do next...

Selina's eyes blinked open. She was vaguely aware of a tingling sensation travelling the length of her spine. Her sleepy gaze rested on Rion and she stretched sensuously across his great body—and felt the growing pressure of his arousal against her thigh. Dream-like, she kissed his broad chest and put out her tongue to lick a dark male nipple, let her fingers edge up into the silken black hair of his head.

She sighed with pleasure, breathing her husband's name, and planted a string of kisses up his throat, tasting his skin. Her small white teeth nipped teasingly at his firm chin and, raising her head, she brushed his lips lightly with her own. Finally she looked up into his eyes, saw the gleam of desire in the black depths. An all-female smile curved her mouth. Rion wanted her...

Rion...

Suddenly Selina was wide awake and aware of where she was—and why. Mortified at what she had done, she placed her hands on his chest to push away from him.

'Don't stop now.' Rion noted the confusion on Selina's face as her body arched back. Sliding an arm around her, he cupped the back of her head in his hand. For an instant she resisted. 'I have never had a pleasanter awakening,' he said huskily, and pulled her head down and captured her mouth, silencing her muffled protest with his.

Her lips opened beneath his and Rion tightened his hand around her taut buttocks, holding her against his pulsing length while his mouth devoured her. His tongue was mimicking what he really wanted, but this time he was determined to go slow and savour her.

Selina hadn't a chance. Her mind and body had already betrayed her and she was hot for him. When he took possession of her mouth a low moan escaped her and she responded with equal fervour.

She didn't protest when he broke the kiss to roll her onto her back. Big and dark, he loomed over her, raking her naked body with hungry eyes, and she revelled in his scrutiny. She lifted her hands to trace the hard planes of his bronzed chest, caressing, and felt him shudder as she stroked lower to his belly.

'Oh, no.' Rion caught her wrists and pinned her arms either side of her body. 'My turn, Selina, my pace,' he rasped and, bending his head, his sensuous mouth found hers and her lips parted eagerly to the erotic penetration of his tongue. They kissed long, deliciously, and finally desperately broke the kiss to breathe. Then with deliberate intent he began a slow seduction of her achingly receptive body.

Selina's breath caught as Rion's lips trailed a path from her mouth to her throat along her collarbone, and for a second time her breath stilled as his head inched lower towards the soft curve of her breast.

With incredible tenderness he kissed a burgeoning peak, opening his mouth to circle the aureole with his tongue before beginning a delicate suckling that pulled like a live wire from her breast to her pelvis, tightening as he continued with an erotic teasing and tasting that was halfway between pleasure and pain. Just when she thought she could stand no more, he moved to bestow a similar torment on its partner. She tried to reach for him, to touch him, but he held her hands firmly at her sides and found her mouth again, kissing her with a hungry passion then trailing kisses over her throat, her shoulders, before inching lower, driving her wild with exquisite pleasure. He inched his way lower still, and wantonly she yielded to the demands of her body and Rion's sensual mastery.

He circled her navel with his tongue, and suddenly her hands were free as he parted her legs. His head dipped to nuzzle at the junction of her thighs, his tongue slipping between the dewy folds to taste her.

Selina had never experienced such intimacy before and, shocked, instinctively reached for his shoulders to push him away. But shock gave way to intense sensual delight, and her slender fingers threaded through his hair, holding him closer.

She was totally oblivious to the guttural cries and moans that escaped her as Rion, with wicked expertise, drew every atom of pleasure from her body until she abandoned herself to the tumultuous waves of sensations rocketing through her slender frame.

Vaguely she heard Rion groan, 'I dreamt of you like this...' and her passion-hazed gaze sought his.

He was kneeling between her thighs, his eyes dark orbs of molten desire, and was lifting her hips. Her body arched like a bow string, her head fell back, and she grabbed at him with desperate hands as with one long, powerful thrust he filled her. Her fingers dug into his shoulders and she clung as he plunged deeper and sent her soaring into the dizzying heights of sensual overload with a white-hot passion that consumed her.

'Yes—oh, yes!' she moaned, her hands grasping, caressing his sweat-slicked satin flesh in a delirium of need as he drove hard and deep, then slowed and stilled, again and again, until finally with one mighty thrust he drove her to the peak of fulfillment and she soared over the edge. His hard, sweat-slicked body bucked and shuddered as he joined her in a sublime explosion of release.

Selina lay beneath him, shaking in the aftermath of passion. Wrapping her arms around his neck, she gloried in his weight, in the erratic thud of his heart against her own as the shudders faded and a hazy glow of repletion enveloped her totally supine body.

It was a low throbbing sound in her head that woke Selina—or was it in her body? Selina thought drowsily, stretching and aching in places she never had before. Slowly she opened her eyes, and was immediately dazzled by the fierce light of the sun shining on her face. Closing them again, she turned away from the blinding light. It was then she realised the throbbing was the sound of the yacht's engine. She was naked in bed, and everything came flooding back.

She stared around at the spaciousness of the master cabin, panelled in walnut with a cleverly built-in closet, a cabinet and a desk. A luxurious sofa and a large chair flanked a polished wood occasional table. The whole effect was elegant and very masculine. As were the navy Egyptian cotton sheets that were rumpled over the enormous bed.

'Oh, God, no,' she groaned.

'Hardly the reception I was hoping for.'

A deep, dark voice laced with amusement echoed in her head.

She opened her eyes again. Rion was standing in the open door, a tray loaded with cups in his hands and the scent of fresh coffee floating in the air. Bare-chested, with khaki shorts riding low on his lean hips, he looked gorgeous, vital and wide awake, while she felt like death.

'You did not say no last night,' Rion drawled and, crossing to the bed, placed the tray on a side table. He sat down on the bed. 'Quite the opposite at one point, I recall,' he said, and chuckled.

'Good morning,' she murmured, ignoring his comment.

Self-loathing was flooding through her at her abject surrender to Rion. But maybe it was to be expected after being celibate for years, she told herself fatalistically. The alternative—that it was only Rion she could not resist—she didn't dare contemplate. She sat up, dragging a sheet with her and tucking it under her armpits. Taking the coffee cup he held out without looking at him, she took a sip and then drained the cup.

'So formal, Selina, and not actually true.' He reached and ran his fingers through the tumbled mass of her hair, smoothing the silken strands back from her shoulders to curl down her spine, sliding his hand down her arm. His touch was light as a feather, creating tiny tremors beneath her skin. 'I thought you needed the rest.'

'What time is it?' she asked and finally glanced at Rion.

She saw the half smile pull at his sensual sculpted mouth, saw the intimate knowledge in his twinkling dark eyes, and her traitorous heart squeezed. The twinkle she had thought long gone was back, and she knew a half-naked smiling Rion was infinitely more dangerous to her emotional health than the ruthless cynical man she knew him to be...

'Noon—but relax.' He took the empty cup from her hand and placed it on the tray. 'Lunch will be served in an hour or so. Plenty of time.' And before she'd realised his intention, he had flipped the sheet down to her waist.

'No, I need a shower,' Selina snapped, and tried to grab the sheet. But he caught her hand in his and held both to her stomach.

As if she had never spoken he continued, 'Last night was great, Selina, but it will be even better now I know what you are capable of.' His free hand reached for her throat, tipping her head back. 'The shy innocent has long gone, and you delighted in seducing me with your sweet mouth…and the rest.'

His hand slid down the soft hollow of her throat and continued its downward journey, brushing the rosy peak of one breast and then with elegant fingers manipulating the tip to pouting hardness.

'Rather like this,' he mocked softly, his fingers playfully walking across to her other breast and delivering the same treatment. 'I appreciate the more experienced Selina, and that innocent blush is quite a clever trick.'

'No!' She was protesting against his assumption and the sensual intent she saw in his dark eyes even as her pulse rate leapt at his wandering hands. 'I didn't know it was you. I was half asleep,' she said without thinking—and knew as soon as the words left her mouth she had said the wrong thing. 'I mean…'

'Too much information, Selina,' he mocked, his lips curving in a sardonic smile as his hand reached up to tangle in her hair, jerking her head towards him. His face was inches from her own. 'This time you will know it is me.' He spoke with a deadly calm that was belied by the barely leashed anger in his dark eyes.

'You don't understand—' she said, but his mouth slammed into hers, kissing her with a domineering savage passion that—humiliatingly—she could not help responding to with an aching need. Then somehow she was on her back and Rion was straddling her, propped up on his strong forearms either side of her body, studying her as if she was some fly under a microscope.

'Your sex education, Selina, while having improved in the physical sense is sadly lacking in etiquette,' he grated. 'First lesson: never tell your partner you were thinking of someone else during sex.'

Selina, her heart racing, heard the inimical anger in his tone, saw his tight mouth and the dull flush on his high cheekbones, and realised too late what she had invited with her careless remark. Rion was hanging on to his fabled control by a thread.

'I never…' She choked incoherently as scorching dark eyes raked over her face, her upturned breasts. Lowering his head, he caught a throbbing peak lightly between his teeth to lash the swelling tip with his tongue. The breath whooshed from her lungs in a gasping groan, warmth pooled between her thighs, and involuntarily her slender hands reached for him.

What followed was a master class.

Selina had had no idea the human body was capable of such unfettered passion…no idea she was capable of behaving like an untamed being, willing to follow Rion's inventive eroticism down pathways she had never dreamt of—until she thought she might pass out from the force of the incredibly emotional storm raging between them.

With his great body over hers, the shuddering tremors finally stopped and Selina opened her eyes, trying to regain control of her erratic breathing and pounding heart. Slowly Rion withdrew and rolled off her. He slipped an arm around her shoulders, his other hand resting across her stomach.

She blushed as she met his dark enigmatic gaze, stunned by what he had done—what she had allowed him to do. She had actually encouraged his sexual manipulation of her body and every one of her senses until that final out-of-this-world orgasm.

'I never...' She couldn't continue, more confused with herself than Rion.

He kissed her damp forehead and smiled a slow, completely masculine grin. 'I rather gathered that—and yet you are an incredibly sensual woman. Admit it, you enjoyed every second. I made sure you did. Maybe because you dented my masculine ego and I wanted to prove a point. I was a little overenthusiastic, but no woman sharing my bed *ever* thinks of another man.'

Such conceit! Selina marveled. But she could well believe it. Rion was an incredible lover. But then he had a lot of practice... She was not his first lover and she certainly would not be his last. Whereas he was her first and only, and she had a growing suspicion he might well be her last. She could not imagine doing with any other man what she had done with Rion. They had joined in the most intimate way possible. They should have been as close as it was possible for two people to be. But sadly Selina realised, with a sense of something precious lost, that Rion was right again. Sex was just sex... two bodies connecting but the mind and heart miles apart.

She glanced down. His bronzed body was perfectly formed, like the Greek god she had once thought him. He was no longer a god in her eyes but a man like any other, with human frailties... Handsome, wealthy and single he could take his pick of women—and frequently did, she had no doubt. Rion had a high libido and enjoyed sex, but he didn't believe in monogamy. He was a chauvinist, and women let him get away with it for the pleasure of his company. And who could blame them? There were much worse vices she knew...

She had been surprised and, being honest, secretly a little pleased that he had actually confessed to having his ego dented by her. And now, held against him, sated with sex, she could not argue with his statement.

She looked up at his face, a dry smile curving her swollen lips. 'You are so arrogant, Rion, and as it happens I *wasn't* thinking of another man last night. I was thinking of you. I was half asleep and thought I was still married,' she said. She saw his smug smile and added, 'But thankfully I woke up from that nightmare...'

The hand on her stomach moved to take her chin between thumb and forefinger, his dark eyes capturing hers. 'You were doing great until the end, Selina. I'll make you pay for that later,' he forewarned her, a slight smile quirking the edges of his mouth. 'Or maybe not,' he amended. 'We could just agree to ignore the past and enjoy the next couple of weeks for what they are—a holiday between two friends.'

Selina's eyes widened. Rion a friend? That would be a first...

'Don't look so shocked.' He chuckled. 'I do *have* friends. Dimitri and Captain Ted have been personal friends of mine for years, and I also keep a friendly relationship with my crew. I do not want them to see us at loggerheads. I run a cheerful ship, and I want it to stay that way. Plus there is no denying sex between us is fantastic.'

She wanted to deny him but it would be a lie, she acknowledged. So much for lying back and thinking of England. Rion looked so attractive with his black hair dishevelled and his handsome face lit with amusement. She felt her heart flutter in her breast. She still wanted him, and this might be the only sex she would ever get…

She had been like a puppy dog lapping up any sign of affection from its master during their brief marriage. But now she worked with captains of industry, billionaires. Some she liked better than others, but she had no problem maintaining a friendly relationship with all of them. A lot of her clients employed her over and over again. Would it be so impossible to develop a friendly relationship with Rion? It would make the next two weeks much easier. She could look on it as a job—which in a way it was… He was paying for it, she reminded herself bluntly.

Stuck on a yacht in the middle of the Mediterranean, she didn't have much of a choice anyway. She could try to resist him but, humiliating as it was to admit, she had spectacularly failed so far. Or she could do as he suggested and try to accept him as a 'friend with benefits.' She believed that was the popular term.

'Yes, why not?' she said just as her stomach gave an almighty rumble.

Rion laughed. 'Great.' He leapt off the bed and pulled on his shorts. 'Come on, Selina, get up,' he commanded. 'You can take that shower and I'll order the food you so obviously need.' And, still chuckling, he turned to walk out of the door.

Without thinking she flung a pillow at him and missed—and heard his laughter as the door swung closed behind him. She rolled off the bed and walked into the *en-suite* bathroom, hardly glancing at the luxury fittings.

Naked, she stepped into the huge shower cubi-

cle and turned on what she hoped was the tap—
only to have jets of water hit her from all sides.
She gulped and blindly reached for the door. She
stepped back out, wiping her hair from her eyes.
She looked around and spotted the bathing ac-
coutrements lined up above a vanity basin. She
glanced at the bottles and jars—all masculine.
So she would smell like Rion. But then she did
already, she thought, and picked up a bottle of
shampoo and padded back to the shower stall.
She eyed the controls, worked out how to turn
on only the overhead sprays, and warily stepped
back inside.

Tipping a dollop of shampoo into her hands,
she quickly washed her hair, and then liberally
anointed her body with shower gel. Finally she
tilted back her head, closed her eyes and let the
powerful spray rinse her hair and her body, trying to rid herself of the tension the pressure of
the past few days had caused.

She raised her hands and ran her fingers
through her hair, smoothing the wet strands from
her face and then lifting her arms high above her

head. She linked her fingers and stretched on tiptoe, easing the ache in muscles she had never known she had…

'Now, *that* is an exquisite sight,' a deep, husky voice growled, and at the same time two large hands cupped her breasts.

She let out a yelp and grasped a pair of strong wrists. A large naked male was at her back. 'You are insatiable.'

'And you love it,' he said huskily. 'Sorry to disappoint you, but you're wrong this time. My turn for the shower.' And, locking his arms around her waist, he swung her out of the cubicle. Catching up a huge towel, he wrapped it around her and briskly rubbed her dry. 'Now, go to your cabin and dress—preferably in the white bikini. Lunch is on the sun deck. I will meet you there in thirty minutes and after that I'll give you a tour of the yacht.'

Back in her cabin, Selina crossed to the closet where she had placed her clothes last night, and withdrew a bra and briefs, a pair of denim shorts and a white tee shirt. She put them on. She was definitely not wearing the white bikini. Rion needed no encouragement, she thought, flushing with shame at the ease with which she had surrendered to him.

Images of his naked body covering hers flashed through her mind. Trying for normality, she picked up her phone and took care of a few essential work queries, then reluctantly left the cabin and ascended the stairs to the main deck. Her hair would dry naturally in the sun—in a curly mess, probably, but she didn't care.

She was here to get an inheritance she had never wanted but now, through no fault of her own, needed. And Rion controlled it, she thought grimly. She had lost her illusions long ago. She was here at his command, as his sexual plaything, and that was all she had to remember...

The weather was perfect. The sun shone in a cloudless sky, glinting off the waves of the azure sea. She could think of plenty of people in worse positions, and her spirits rose. She should be thankful for what she had. What was two weeks out of her life? A mere blip.

A small, dark-eyed young man appeared, with a heavy-laden tray in his hands. He introduced himself as Marco and offered to show her the way to the sun deck with a broad smile on his face. She smiled back and chatted easily to him as he led her up three levels to the sun deck. Her eyes widened in surprise on a plunge pool and a Jacuzzi set on one side of the deck. Maybe that was why Rion had told her to wear her bikini? Too late now.

She glanced down at a low table, set with cutlery, condiments, glasses and an ice bucket containing a bottle of wine. 'I could have eaten on the main deck, Marco, and saved you the walk,' she said, smiling. 'I will next time.'

Rion reached the top of the stairs from the wheelhouse and paused to catch his breath—not from lack of energy but at the picture Selina presented. Wearing brief denim shorts and a tee shirt, with flip-flops on her feet, she was talking to Marco. A brilliant smile curved her soft mouth, her eyes were shining and her glorious hair shimmered like beaten gold in the sun.

'No, you won't.' Rion walked forward. 'I decide where we eat.' It was callous of him, but he had heard what she said, and seeing Selina smiling at young Marco had hit a nerve...

Selina glanced back to where Rion stood. He had showered, shaved and changed into a checked open-necked shirt and another pair of khaki shorts. He looked vitally attractive and as bossy as ever...

'Yes, oh, master,' she mocked, and turned to smile at Marco again before sinking down on a carefully placed lounger.

Marco put a bowl of salad, bread, a platter of delicious-looking seafood and another of various meats on the table.

'You are learning, sweetheart,' Rion drawled. 'But where is the bikini?'

'I forgot,' she said. 'Sorry.' And gave him a saccharine smile.

His dark eyes were openly laughing at her little rebellion. With one hand he deftly unfastened a few more buttons of his shirt and sank down onto a lounger, stretching his long legs out before him in negligent ease.

'Thanks, Marco. I'll pour the wine.' Rion dismissed him.

'Iris was right to call you Old Bossy Boots. I should have listened to her,' Selina opined, and reached forward. Taking a plate, she piled on salad, prawn, langoustines and crusty bread. Fish first, meat second, she thought. 'What is Iris doing now?' she asked idly, popping a prawn in her mouth and forking up some salad as Rion poured the chilled white wine into two glasses.

'She is married to an Australian of Greek descent and living on the Gold Coast in Australia. They have a son, and are expecting the arrival of their second child any day now. Helen is in her element as doting grandmother, and spends a lot of her time there,' he told her, piling his own plate high with assorted meats and salad and starting to eat.

'What about your father?' she asked in between mouthfuls of food. 'I bet he spoils the boy rotten.'

Rion put down his knife and fork and shot her a hard look. 'No, my father never got the chance. He died five years ago. Not unexpected. He knew his heart was damaged and his time limited.'

'I'm so sorry. I know how close you were. It must have been hard, losing him,' Selina said softly.

'Drop the false sympathy, *pethi mou*,' Rion drawled. The endearment was an echo from the past but with a sardonic emphasis. 'You are more likely to dance on his grave. I know your grandfather must have told you that my father made a deal with him to buy Stakis Shipping that included you.' He elevated one shoulder in a negligent shrug, but his strong face hardened. 'It was to be his last big deal before he retired—supposedly his final success. He enjoyed a world cruise and died a couple of months after he returned. End of story.' Picking up his knife and fork, Rion resumed eating.

So did Selina…but something about the information was disturbing her. She was not sure it was the end of the story. 'If your father—' she began.

'Enough, Selina.' Rion cast her an impatient glance. 'Talk of the past is out, remember?' Draining his wine glass, he rose to his feet. 'Now, if you are finished eating, I'll show you around the yacht.'

Selina finished a langoustine, refusing to be hurried, and glanced up at him through the veil of her lashes. Big and boldly handsome, Rion was a live wire, full of restless driven energy. He always had been, Selina realised, and always would be. He worked hard and played hard and rarely stopped. No woman would ever tie him down.

She glanced around at the fantastic view and rose to her feet with a shake of her head. 'Yes, okay—lead on.' Rion was incapable of relaxing. 'Though I'm surprised you like cruising. Days at sea with nothing to do but admire the view does not seem like you.'

A glint of humour flashed in Rion's eyes. 'I love the sea.' He let his gaze slide blatantly down the length of her body and back. 'And the view,' he quipped with a heart-stopping sensuous smile that made her breath quicken. 'But you are right. I worked for a while this morning—I do every day.'

Why did his brilliant white smile suddenly remind Selina of a predatory panther?

'Then I relax in the afternoon—sometimes in the pool. But as you have forgotten your bikini, your loss is my gain.' And he kissed her and took her back to bed.

Eventually Rion did take her on a tour of the yacht, and introduced her to Captain Ted—an Englishman—who made her feel at ease by saying, 'Rion told me an old friend was joining the cruise and I imagined another Dimitri. It is a real pleasure to meet you and a relief—you are a thousand times better to look at.' He grinned. 'Anything you need, just ask me.'

'Down, Ted,' Rion said dryly, slipping an arm around Selina's waist. 'The lady is my guest and *I* will provide everything she needs.'

As he led her away from the bridge for a moment it crossed Selina's mind Rion that might be jealous, but she instantly dismissed the thought.

She enjoyed the rest of the tour. She might have been overawed by the *Theodora*, a beautiful, luxuriously fitted vessel, with five guest cabins, a formal and an informal salon, but her job had on occasion taken her on yachts even larger and more blatantly luxurious. None had been as eclectically fitted out with a mixture of traditional and new, and meeting the crew and seeing the way they worked she recognised the easy, friendly atmosphere on the *Theodora* was not something she had ever felt on the bigger yachts she had travelled on. She was quietly impressed.

CHAPTER SEVEN

BACK in her own cabin, Selina showered again and, slipping on silk briefs and a bra, looked at the few clothes in the closet. She had not brought a large suitcase, so she had none of the smart suits and gowns she needed to blend in with the upper echelons of society the majority of her clients inhabited to choose from. She had only a small suitcase, containing toiletries, towels, her sweatsuit, a sweater, a swimsuit, a bikini and underwear, the black silk dress she had worn for the funeral plus two summer dresses—one blue and one yellow, which had the advantage of being crease-resistant and could fold up into the size of a man's hanky—two shirts, two tee shirts and two pretty tops, a pair of smart white linen pants, denim shorts, a pair of flip-flops, black high heels and a pair of sandals.

She flicked through the closet and took out the yellow dress, eyeing the black one she had worn for the funeral and the stiletto heels. She slipped the yellow dress over her head. After applying some moisturiser to her face she brushed her hair, put on her sandals, and left the cabin.

Nervously Selina entered the main salon, feeling like a scarlet woman—but in yellow... Rion, looking wickedly attractive in white pants and a white shirt, crossed to take her arm.

'You look lovely,' he said huskily, and offered her a drink as he led her across to join Dimitri and Captain Ted at the bar.

Selina took a sip of the martini she had requested and began to relax. After she discovered over the pre-dinner drinks that Ted's parents lived in Weymouth, not far from her home, she did not feel such an alien in the all-male company and relaxed a little more.

Dinner was a casual affair. Marco presented the wine and filled all the glasses, then served the food, which was superb. Not surprisingly, with three men present the conversation got around to cars. Selina sipped at her wine and listened. Apparently Rion had recently bought a Bugatti Veyron, whatever that was, and the discussion of its merits went right over her head. She drained her glass. Then Ted said he was thinking of buying a new Mercedes.

Selina grinned. 'You must have been to that Mercedes dealership, Ted—the one with the museum and training track in Weymouth. It is a great place. A friend took me and I got a new Mercedes there—the small fourteen hundred. It took two months to be delivered and I collected it…' she paused to think; her schedule had been so messed up '…ten days ago. I love it—though I only got the chance to drive it a couple of times before I had to come to Greece,' she said ruefully.

'Surely a family funeral takes precedence over a car?' Rion opined. 'Unlike your grandfather, the car will still be there when you get back.'

She looked at Rion, seated at the head of the table, and caught an expression of cold contempt on his hard face. What had she supposedly done wrong now? Not that she cared.

'Yes, of course,' she responded. And fortified by wine added, 'That is, providing Aunt Peggy, who is driving the car while I am away, has not run into anything again. She wrote off my Beetle in a car park.'

Ted and Dimitri laughed, and Rion smiled, but she saw no humour in his eyes.

Although the food was excellent Selina had lost her appetite—or maybe it was the wine—and she was glad when the meal ended. She made her excuses to leave before coffee was served. Not that it made any difference. Rion followed her and overrode any resistance she attempted with an ease that shamed but aroused her—and she still ended up in his big bed.

That day set the pattern for the following days. They ate lunch and dinner together—Rion was a good conversationalist, and they discussed a variety of subjects but never the past—and they had sex every night in his vast bed.

She never actually spent a night in her own bed. Rion worked in the morning and after lunch they enjoyed a *siesta* of sorts but with little real intimacy—which suited Selina fine.

Four days later Selina stood impatiently on the deck and watched Rion, wearing a black wet-suit that revealed in intimate detail the physical perfection of his great body, check all his diving equipment for the final time. She had never known Rion liked scuba-diving, nor that Dimitri was here for that express purpose until dinner two nights ago, when she had discovered the main reason for the cruise was a diving expedition the two men had arranged to explore sites off the coast of Egypt.

Satisfied everything was ready, Rion walked across to where Selina was waiting so impatiently. The baggy sweater she wore did not stop him from appreciating her lithe body and fabulous legs.

'I'm still not sure about this,' he said, looking down into her sparkling eyes and seeing the excitement there. She had asked him to let her go on a dive yesterday. Surprised that she *could* dive he'd said no, and that there was no suit to fit her anyway. Then apparently Dimitri had found an old suit in the locker, and she had caught Rion at a weak moment in bed last night and he had agreed. 'Tell me again where you qualified as a diver.' His mind had been on another sport last night.

'I told you—I was a member of the school diving club, and then when I finished university I spent six months travelling in the Far East. I took my Diving Masters on a ten-week course in Queensland, Australia. I have my Paddy certificate. Now, can I suit up?'

'Okay. But understand *I* am the master on this dive.'

'Yes, of course—aren't you always?' she said, and wrinkled her nose at him.

Her enthusiasm was infectious.

Rion was beginning to realise everything about Selina was infectious.

Everyone on board adored her—from the oldest to the youngest. Dimitri and Ted, the most reserved of men, could not keep their eyes off her and nor could Marco, who had previously worn the suit that Selina was wearing today.

The thought of a suit that had been plastered to young Marco's body in equally intimate contact with Selina's was somehow distasteful to him. Why, Rion wasn't sure—in fact where Selina was concerned he wasn't sure of anything any more. For a woman who wore designer clothes and casually admitted that an obviously male friend had bought her a Mercedes, she happily walked around the yacht wearing a pair of old denim shorts and a shirt. She never wore make-up, the only cream he had ever seen her use was sunblock, and with her glorious hair piled on top of her head with a rubber band and flip-flops on her dainty feet she looked like Orphan Annie...a very sexy orphan Annie.

All the previous female guests on his yacht he could remember had invariably worn full make-up and stretched out on the sun deck wearing the briefest of bikinis or even just a thong, advertising their attributes to Rion and the whole crew. Selina, on the other hand, when she did go in the pool, wore a black sports costume—sexy, but not the bikini that he fantasised about. And she never sunbathed. He would usually find her sitting in the shade with a book or on her phone. She was the least vain woman Rion had ever known—which didn't sit well with his opinion of her as a devious, greedy woman who used her physical assets and talents to enjoy the high life.

Looking down at her as she peeled off her sweater, his dark eyes flared and his breath stopped in his throat. She was wearing the white bikini, with those tempting little ribbons holding it together, and instantly he could feel his erection straining uncomfortably beneath his wetsuit. Every thought left his head except the one telling him he needed to get in the water fast or disgrace himself.

Over an hour later, back on board with her wetsuit stripped off, Selina kneeled on the deck and emptied her net of finds on the polished wood. She spotted a small encrusted lump with a glint of gold on one side and picked it up. She glanced over her shoulder at Rion, sprawled in a lounger a few feet away.

'Look, Rion—I'm sure this must be gold. A coin...maybe a doubloon from a pirate ship?' She stretched her arm back, holding it out for him to see. 'What do you think?' she demanded, excited by her find.

Rion thought she had incredible sparkling eyes, a vivid imagination, and was slightly mad... Madly beautiful... With her bum in the air and her body half twisted towards him she gave him a shockingly tempting view of one perfect breast almost falling out of the tiny triangle of white material.

'I think we should take it down to the lab, get it cleaned and see.'

What he actually thought was that he wanted to take her inside and ravish her. She was driving him crazy. He had never dived with a woman partner before—never considered it—but Selina had amazed him. She was good—very good—except for a tendency to dive down and pick up any old junk off the seabed. Watching her sleek body in the water had been a bit like water torture for him…

Until today Rion would have sworn it was impossible to be aroused thirty feet under water…

There was another certainty gone…

'Great—just wait until I pick up the rest.' Selina turned to put her other finds back in the net.

'No, just take the coin.' Rion got to his feet and strode over to her. 'The sun will dry the rest out.' And with a bit of luck blow it away!

'Good idea.' Selina sprang to her feet with her find in her hand. 'It was wonderful today. Thank you for taking me.' She grinned.

He smiled—a wry curve of his sensual lips. 'My pleasure.' Well, not quite. He intended it to be. But he didn't make the crack that hovered on his tongue. She reminded him of the girl he had first met—so innocent, her face flushed with pleasure…

He led her below deck to the diving lab, where any finds were examined and placed in a locker.

Ten minutes later Selina looked in awe at the coin Rion held in the palm of his hand. 'What do you think? Is it Egyptian? Greek? Or maybe Spanish?' she asked excitedly.

'It is definitely Greek—and now I want my reward for cleaning it,' Rion said huskily. Watching her jump up and down with pleasure in her white bikini was killing him.

'Can I hold it? Is it really ancient?'

Unaware of Rion's problem, Selina felt excitement fizzing through her as she glanced from the coin in his hand up into Rion's dark face. Only then did she see the banked-down desire and something else…an echo from the past in his expression…that made her excitement level rise even further.

'I'll look it up later,' he said, and dropped the coin on the steel table. His dark eyes holding hers, he curved an arm around her waist to pull her close. 'Right now I have a more pressing problem I need to deal with. The vision of you in this bikini has been haunting me for a week,' he breathed against Selina's lips, tempting but not touching, running a long finger beneath the fine strap of her top.

Selina's breath caught at the feel of his hard, hot body against her, stirring her blood and melting her bones, and she couldn't speak, could only stare as Rion stepped back and pulled off his khaki shorts. She gasped at the sheer strength of his arousal.

'I can't wait,' he murmured, and he flicked the clasp between her breasts and peeled the scrap of material over her shoulders and down her arms to fall to the floor.

She let him, excitement riding her. His hands clasped her waist and he bent his head to brush her lips with his, moving lower to draw one pouting nipple into his mouth, suckling then delivering the same treatment to the other. While his hands stroked over her hips his fingers deftly unfastened the two tiny ribbons that held the fabric that protected her modesty. He pulled the slip of material between her legs and dropped it on the table.

Selina saw his face, a taut mask of raw passion, and shuddered in eager response as in one deft movement his strong hands lifted her onto the table, wrapped her legs around his waist and thrust into her already moist, waiting body. She grasped his arms, his shoulders, her fingernails digging into his flesh as he possessed her with an uncontrollable driven hunger, and she convulsed around him, shuddering violently as he climaxed with her.

He folded his arms round her and rested his head against hers for long minutes, until finally the lingering waves of release faded away and they could breathe again.

'I didn't—'

'Don't say a word. Just lift me off here,' Selina said huskily.

Rion lifted her up and slowly lowered her to the ground. 'Are you okay?'

She looked at him naked, and then at herself, a wobbly rueful smile curving her swollen lips. 'I'm not complaining, and I'll be fine if I can find my bikini.'

Selina glanced around the room, her eyes scanning the tabletop and spotting the lower half of her bikini. She picked it up and tied it back on.

Wordlessly Rion retrieved her top and his shorts from the floor and pulled his shorts on. What could he say after ravishing her on a metal tabletop? That he never lost control? Well, that was a lie. He had—quite spectacularly. He handed her the top…

Selina took it and slipped it on. Feeling better dressed, she looked around again, her smooth brow creasing in a frown as she scanned the long table a second time. Eventually she turned back to Rion and placed her hands on her hips, indignant amber eyes clashing with his.

'I will kill you, Rion Moralis, if you have lost my coin. You put it on the table and I can't see it anywhere now.'

Rion couldn't help it. He burst out laughing…

'It is not funny. The coin might be a valuable find—very ancient. You said it was Greek.'

'It is. But it is not gold and not very old,' he said, grinning down at her. 'It is a fifty-drachma coin from nineteen-ninety, and no longer any use because the Greek currency changed to the euro in two thousand and one.'

Selina was crushed 'Really?' She looked up into Rion's laughing eyes. 'You knew before we—'

'Sorry. Yes. But you were so excited I didn't want to disillusion you.'

'You mean until you had your wicked way with me?' She grinned up at him.

Rion swept her up in his arms. 'What can I say? A man needs to do what a man needs to do.' He buried his head in her glorious hair and, biting his lip to stop laughing, carried her to her cabin and lowered her gently to her feet. 'Take a rest before dinner, Selina, you have had a strenuous day.' And, planting a swift kiss on the tip of her nose, he walked out, still grinning broadly.

'You look happy,' Dimitri said as he strolled into the main salon and poured himself a whisky from the bar.

'I am,' he said, glancing at his old friend who

was sitting having his usual whisky and soda. He realised he actually *was*. He hadn't felt this good in ages. Raising his glass, he took a swig of whisky. 'It was a great dive and Selina really surprised me. She is very good.'

'What happened with the gold lump she recovered from the seabed?'

Rion grinned and told him.

Dimitri started to chuckle, then laughed out loud. 'I bet Selina was disappointed it wasn't the treasure she thought she had found.'

'No, she took it quite well—she saw the funny side,' Rion corrected him.

'Yes, she would,' Dimitri said, more seriously. 'Selina is an incredible girl—just the sort you should marry. If I was single and twenty years younger I'd marry her myself.'

A sharp stab of anger twisted Rion's gut at the mention of marriage. Selina was hot in bed but he would never forget she had betrayed him.

'That's never going to happen. She is my ex-wife.'

Dimitri choked on his whisky.

* * *

Selina awoke to a loud whirring noise and turned her head. The impression of Rion's head on the pillow was the only sign he had been in the bed, but stretching her body reminded her. At dinner last night Dimitri and Ted had delighted in teasing her about the coin she had found, and finally Rion had decided they needed an early night. They had retired to bed, where they had indulged their sexual appetite to the full, and now he had gone—not that Selina was complaining. She had been with him all the way and was exhausted. Glancing at the bedside clock, she groaned.

It was only five in the morning. As the noise got louder she rolled over onto her stomach and pulled a pillow over her head to block out the sound. She needed her sleep. It would be nice to wake up in her own bed for a change—she never had so far…

The next time she opened her eyes she saw Rion, dressed in his usual khaki shorts and a white open-necked shirt, his hair still wet from the shower. He looked disgustingly fit and devilishly attractive. 'What time is it?' she asked. And, not waiting for an answer, said, 'A terrible noise woke me up at five this morning. You had gone. What was it?' She assumed he had gone to investigate.

'Nothing to worry about and it is now ten.' Handing her a cup of coffee, he added, 'Drink this and then get dressed. I have a surprise for you.'

He put his hand in his shorts' pocket and handed her a coin.

She turned it over and saw the date: nineteen-ninety. 'You *are* joking?'

Rion leant over and dropped a brief kiss on her parted lips. 'I thought you might like to have it as a keepsake.'

'Very funny. I am never going to live this down—and if that is the surprise, I am not impressed,' she said, but grinned and put the coin on the side table.

'No, that is not the surprise. When you are ready meet me at the diving station.'

* * *

Round-eyed, Selina looked at the new red-trimmed black wetsuit and saw it was her size. Then she looked up at the two men standing watching her, both with broad grins on their faces.

'I love it! Thank you.' She stretched up and flung her arms around Rion's neck and kissed his cheek. 'But where did you get it from, out here in the middle of the sea?'

'The noise you heard last night was a helicopter. I had it flown in from Cyprus.'

'What...?' she exclaimed, taking a step back. For Rion to go to so much trouble for her was incredible—and then another thought struck her. 'That helicopter must have cost a fortune. With all the needy people in the world tell me you didn't waste all that money just for a wetsuit? The old one was fine,' she remonstrated.

'No, of course not,' Rion replied, and Dimitri cut in.

'The helicopter was delivering essential supplies and more oxygen tanks. The wetsuit was just added to the list. Try it for size and then you and Rion can get a dive in—about forty-five minutes, okay?'

'Oh, great.' Selina grinned. 'I don't have to feel guilty.'

Apart from being teased by just about everyone on board about her so-called find the day before, today had been perfect, Selina thought later that evening when, wearing the blue silk dress, she joined Rion, Ted and Dimitri for dinner in the main salon.

The conversation was mostly about diving, and Dimitri made her laugh when he recounted some of his experiences as a diving instructor. Selina was surprised to learn he had known Rion since he was a boy, and had actually taught Rion's mother Theodora, whom the yacht was named after, to dive. Selina had assumed the yacht was named after some woman Rion had known, and though she was loath to admit it she was relieved to know she was wrong.

Apparently Dimitri, who was also a qualified geologist, had worked as a diving instructor in

Greece in his twenties, and then when he'd met his wife, who was South American, had moved to Brazil and started his own diving school there. It had become highly successful and now his eldest son ran it so Dimitri had the time to concentrate on exploration. He read old literature on wrecks and, using his geology skills in studying the seabed, was hoping to find some evidence of them, if not the actual wrecks.

'So that is why you spent most of today's dive with your camera and stopped me from picking anything up,' Selina prompted, grinning at Rion.

'Something like that, sweetheart,' Rion said, with an amused smile that made the men grin.

She had no idea why. But the endearment and the tenderness she heard in his voice stole her breath away.

Later there was no thought of sleep as they lay in the big bed, naked limbs entwined, flesh on flesh, exploring and encouraging, bodies moving in perfect rhythm as they found the highest pinnacle of pleasure.

The following two days went by much the

same. Rion restricted her to one dive a day, and though she never found anything significant, she didn't mind. Much as she loved scuba-diving, she found she was also enjoying the leisure time. Usually she was an early riser—seven at the latest—but now she slept until nine or later. Whether it was the exercise, the lifestyle of sun, sea and sex, she didn't analyse. She simply took each day as it came and was surprisingly content to do so.

But in the darkest corner of her mind a warning voice told her it was far too good to last. This casually dressed, caring and friendly Rion was not the real Rion—the ruthless business tycoon who had cut her out of his life without a word—and she was in grave danger of living in a fool's paradise if she let herself believe otherwise.

CHAPTER EIGHT

SELINA wasn't sure what or who had woken her and languidly she turned her head, resting her eyes on Rion. He was lying flat on his back, one long arm stretched across the top of the pillow behind her head, the other flung out across the bed, palm-up, long fingers loosely curled. His broad chest rose and fell. He was deeply asleep.

He had made wonderful love to her—slowly, tenderly, laughing, talking and teasing. She had unthinkingly commented that she had never re-alised a honeymoon could be such fun, and he had made amazing love to her again until, ex-hausted, they had slept.

Raising a hand, she lightly brushed back a lock of black hair from his brow. In sleep he looked younger, the long, thick black lashes edging his cheekbones concealing the cynical hardness that she had noticed in his eyes when they met again.

Since their first dive together, she mused, there had been no trace of hardness when her eyes met his, but an ease and humour—even gentleness. Against all the odds given their mutual past and the reason she was here, she felt as if they had developed a friendship of equals.

In the depths of the sea, moving among a myriad of aquatic life in a kaleidoscope of colours and shapes as diving buddies, it was magical. The correct signals were instinctive but almost superfluous. They were so attuned to each other—perfect partners. Over meals with the others, or amid the talk and laughter during the day, she was always conscious of the underlying sensual awareness between them. She sensed it in a light touch on her arm, saw it in a look, a certain gleam in his eyes. She knew it meant Rion always wanted to make love to her.

No, he didn't. There was no love involved…

She tried to remind herself of that and realised it was becoming much harder for her to believe that the passion they shared was basic sex. True for Rion, yes…she had known that from the day she had seen him with those other women, heard the comments about him on video…

In a cruel moment of self-awareness she knew she could no longer fool herself that it was true for her. The ache in her heart growing with every breath she took, she stared through the darkness and finally accepted her own truth.

She loved Rion—probably always had…

Lying next to him in the vast bed, she squeezed back the tears that threatened. She had cried an ocean of tears over Rion six years ago, and she knew she had to get away before she broke down and humiliated herself by doing the same again.

Tentatively she edged away from the warmth of his big body. He wasn't holding her, but she felt him stir and froze for an instant then moved again making sure to miss his arm across the top of her pillow. Finally she slid out of bed.

Uncaring that she was naked, she quietly fled back to her own cabin.

Selina closed the door behind her and with legs

like lead crossed the room to flop face-down on the bed.

She couldn't and wouldn't put herself through the agony and humiliation of loving Rion again. But she felt the pressure building up inside her, the pain she was helpless to prevent, and silent tears of anguish filled her eyes before running down her pale cheeks. A low moan escaped her as she felt the salty taste of tears on her lips.

Hating her own weakness, she rubbed the tears away with a fist and rolled over onto her back. She gazed sightlessly at the ceiling, her mind churning with memories she would never forget.

Why, oh, why had she put her head in the same noose twice? she asked herself. She was not a teenager any more with a head full of romantic dreams of a soul mate, a husband, a family. She was a twenty-four-year-old career woman who had learnt more about the sordid side of life than she could ever have imagined, and in her own small way was trying to do something to improve the lives of others a lot less fortunate than her.

So she loved Rion, and she would have to live with that knowledge to her dying day, she thought bleakly. It changed nothing...

She slid off the bed and walked into the bathroom. Turning on the shower, she stood under the soothing spray. She still had her work, her purpose in life, and she still had to get through a few more days with Rion. She hated him for what he had done to her before, and yet paradoxically still loved him. He must never find out.

She turned off the shower and stepped out, drying herself with a large towel. She walked back into the room and glanced at the bed. No—lying down was not an option. In sleep the dreams would come, and she did not need that. She pulled on a bra and pants and padded back into the bathroom. Taking the hair dryer from the wall, she methodically dried her long hair. Then she returned to the bedroom. Pulling on her denim shorts, she slipped a black tee shirt over her head and crossed to the table. She sat down on the sofa and picked up her phone, surprised to see it was six in the morning.

She would have to face Rion soon, and she realised that to retain her pride and dignity everything must seem the same. She must behave the same. Five days left…could she do it? Yes, she had to…and then when the time came she would get the money for the shares and with her head held high walk away and never look back.

She'd wait an hour or so. A buffet breakfast was set out every morning from seven until ten by Louis, the French chef. She would make an appearance at seven. In the meantime, after answering a few e-mails she would contact Beth. They were about twelve hours ahead in the Far East—early evening was a good time to catch her.

Talking to Beth reminded Selina of the good in her normal life. She told Beth she was enjoying her holiday, and had been on a scuba-diving trip with a few others on the cruise and it had been great. Not exactly a lie. She simply omitted the fact it was a private yacht. Then she listened to her friend's news, the latest successes, and hearing about the antics of the children lifted Selina's spirits. She promised Beth she would see her in seven or eight days' time and would stay three weeks before flying on to Australia to meet a client, and then rang off.

Popping her phone into the pocket of her shorts, she determinedly left the cabin to face the day and Rion.

She wandered into the salon, where the breakfast buffet was laid out. It was empty except for Louis, and she helped herself to a mug of fresh-ground coffee. She told him she was going to eat outside and reached for one of his delicious pastries, but he insisted he would serve her.

The main salon opened onto a semi-circular lounging area, with big soft cream leather seats arranged to follow the curve and a circular table in the centre. A tinted-glass retractable roof protected the furnishings without impeding on the view.

Selina took a long swallow of coffee and glanced around the empty deck and then out to the sea, glistening in the early-morning sun. Placing her cup on the table, she sat down.

'*Voilá!*' Louis appeared with a tray laden with exquisite pastries and placed it on the table with a flourish.

'Louis, you are spoiling me—I only wanted one.' She smiled. 'I'll get fat if I eat any more.'

In a Gallic gesture he flung his hands wide. 'Ah Selina, *ma chére*, a woman as beautiful as you deserves to be spoilt. Trust me... I am a connoisseur of women and you are not the type to ever get fat.'

'And *you* are an incorrigible flirt.' She grinned.

'Yes, he is,' a deep voice drawled, and Selina glanced up as Rion sank down beside her. 'Bring me a coffee please, Louis,' he added as he slid his hand around the back of her neck and kissed her.

She dissolved at his touch, and knew without a shadow of a doubt she still loved him.

'That's better,' Rion breathed, raising his head. 'What happened to you? My bed was empty when I woke up.'

'*You* happened. You were spread-eagle across the bed and I almost fell out, so I got up, intending to get in the other side, then remembered I wanted to call Beth and my phone was in my cabin. She is in the Far East, and with the time difference I was able to catch her. Plus, as we are going on a dive this morning, I needed the rest.' She knew she was babbling, but could not help herself.

Rion sat back. He didn't need reminding of Beth. Her father had been Selina's divorce lawyer. But he was not in the mood to argue. He had other things on his mind—the possibility of a great deal going belly-up. But he was not about to let that happen.

He'd had a meeting scheduled for nine days' time in Athens, with the owner of an American company who had offered Rion the chance to buy his company at a price to be agreed. This morning the man had contacted him to cancel, saying he had changed his schedule and would not be going to Greece after all. He would be in Malta for the next three days with his wife, then she was returning to the USA. He had further business in the Far East—maybe they could re-schedule the meeting there?

Rion guessed the man was having second thoughts about selling, but knew it was too good a deal to miss. His mind was filtering through all the possibilities.

'So you still keep in touch? That's nice,' he said rather belatedly to Selina. 'But about the dive…I will not have time today—something has come up and I need to work on it. I'll get Dimitri to partner you.'

Selina recognised the distant look in his eyes from old. Rion was here, but his brilliant mind was miles away. The warning voice in the darkest reaches of her mind rang loud and clear but too late. It had been too good to last. She had been right to be wary. Rion had not changed. Work was his great interest—scuba-diving and sex his relaxation.

He proved it that night at dinner. The yacht was sailing on to the last diving site, where they were due to stay for two days before cruising back to

Greece. But over the meal, as the conversation turned to the next day's dive, Rion said that unfortunately it would have to be the last. They were sailing on to Malta as soon as the dive was done tomorrow. Captain Ted had plotted a course so they would arrive in Malta late the next afternoon, and Rion had a meeting to attend in the capital, Valletta.

Selina's eyes rested on Rion at the head of the table.

'Just like that we are going to Malta?' she snapped, still shaken and confused by the realisation that she loved Rion, and angry at him because he wasn't worth her love, and angry at herself for her weakness…

His jaw tightened and his hard eyes met hers. She could tell he did not like being challenged.

'Unavoidable, I'm afraid,' he said smoothly. 'I have a company to run and it takes precedence over everything else.'

'Yes, of course,' she said, with a hint of sarcasm… She was not in the least surprised. She knew just how persistent Rion could be in business. He had wealth and power and a single-minded ruthless determination to get his own way—a combination almost impossible to beat. He had married her and divorced her all in the name of business...now he had virtually blackmailed her into his bed. She could not see what benefit it was to him businesswise, but she would not be surprised if it was!

'You will like Malta, Selina. I have it on good authority the shopping is excellent.'

His condescending tone infuriated her.

'I know. I have been there,' she said, anger and resentment swirling around inside her. His 'good authority' was one of his women, probably.

'Not that surprising. Malta is a very popular holiday destination with the English, I believe.'

'I wasn't on holiday. I was working for an Arab sheikh,' she shot back. 'He was a generous man and gave me a lot of free time.'

Something ugly moved in his black eyes, but no hint of emotion disturbed the sharp angles of his handsome face. 'Good for you.'

'Yes, it was *very* good. I got to go diving off

the island of Gozo.' She tore her gaze away from Rion to glance across the table at Dimitri. 'You should try it, Dimitri, if you have not already. The rock formation from the island and deep into the sea is fascinating, and the number of wrecks is amazing—from ancient times to the Second World War.'

Dimitri grinned at her. 'No, I haven't. But if we get there early enough maybe you can show me, as Rion will be otherwise occupied?'

'I'd be delighted to,' Selina agreed.

'Forget it,' Rion commanded, and frowned.

The moment he had seen Selina walk into the room he had sensed something different about her. Gone were the blue and yellow dresses she habitually wore, with their gently curved necklines so neatly styled to skim her figure. Instead she was wearing tailored white pants that clung to her hips and thighs and a skimpy green top, and she was wearing make-up for the first time since coming on board.

His frown deepened. She looked stunning, with the creamy curves of her breasts revealed by the silk top and her hair flowing in soft waves over her shoulders, and bore little resemblance to the Orphan Annie persona he had come to know and like. Was he disappointed? No. Selina was as he had thought when he'd met her again: the same as every other foxy female he had known, adopting an age-old ploy to try and arouse his jealousy by deliberately baiting him. Probably because he had been working most of the day and she had been deprived of his attention. She was flirting with Dimitri and his old friend was encouraging her for devilment, he knew. But Rion was never jealous, and no woman ever distracted him from his work, so he refused to rise to the bait.

'When we arrive in Malta I doubt there will be enough light to allow you to travel to Gozo and dive. Plus I have invited an American couple for dinner and you will need to be prepared to meet them. Sorry, Selina—another time, perhaps.'

Selina's eye rested on Rion. The supercilious swine wasn't sorry at all. 'No need to apologise—it does not matter. I get plenty of opportunities in my line of work.' She smiled sweetly at him and resumed eating, letting the conversation flow around her.

Why she loved Rion she could not imagine. He was the most arrogant, overbearing man she had ever met—and she had met a few. Some even wealthier than Rion and, if she was being dispassionate about it, some better-looking. The Arab sheikh for one had been the most classically beautiful man she had ever seen, and surprisingly nice. He was very happily married—albeit with four wives—but had told her if he'd had a vacancy he would have married her...

The rest of the meal was a tense affair. Selina felt her nerves tighten every time she glanced up and met Rion's dark, impenetrable gaze. She was glad when the meal was over, and refused to join the men on deck for a nightcap.

'Goodnight,' she said, and left.

Back in her cabin, she stripped off her clothes. Feeling vulnerable, she had put on a little make-up and dressed differently to give her confidence a boost. Now, as she removed her make-up with a cleansing wipe and walked into the *en-suite* bathroom, she wondered why she'd bothered. She piled her hair up and tucked it under a shower cap, then turned on the water and took a quick shower. Stepping back out, she dried herself, pulled off the shower cap and shook her hair out. She slipped on the towelling robe provided, and tied the belt loosely around her waist.

Sighing, she walked back into the bedroom—and froze. Rion was standing by the table, her phone in his hand.

'What are you doing with that?' she demanded, dashing across to him and grasping at her phone. 'That is my private property and you have no right to touch it.'

'I heard you in the shower and answered it for you,' he said, with the arch of an ebony brow. 'Someone called Trevor wanted you to confirm your date of arrival.'

Rion was angry. His expression was bland, but

she could tell by the glitter in his eyes and the tension in his huge body.

'I will later,' she shot back, and shoved the phone in the pocket of her robe.

But Rion was not finished.

'I told him I didn't know the exact date but that you were my cruising companion for the next four days, if that helped.'

'Oh, hell!' she exclaimed.

As Rion reached for the belt of her robe, she batted his hand away in her agitation and glared furiously up at him.

'What on earth did you say that for?'

'I told him the truth. Something you seem reluctant to do. You seem nervous, Selina. Does Trevor believe he is your only lover?' he queried cynically.

'Don't be ridiculous. Just tell me you did not give him your name.'

'As it happens, no, I didn't.' His stormy eyes narrowed on her flushed, furious face. 'The poor devil was so shocked you were with another man he never asked me. In fact he actually apologised for disturbing you and hung up. But why does my name matter?' he demanded curtly.

'Isn't that obvious? I don't want anyone knowing I am with you,' she fired back. 'Certainly not Trevor, as he happens to be Beth's husband. I have already lied to Anna, and told Aunt Peggy and Beth I'm on a holiday cruise around the Mediterranean with hundreds of other passengers. Beth will have a million questions when she hears I am with a man. Thank God she does not know it is you. She hates you.'

'I'm not that fond of her either,' Rion said dryly, and reaching for her shoulders pulled her closer. 'But you—now, that is a different matter, Selina.' And he dipped his head and brushed her lips with his.

She shivered, intensely aware she was naked beneath the robe, and glancing up saw the gleam in his eyes. Where had his anger gone? With his white shirt open to reveal the strong column of his throat he looked dangerously sexy and very sure of himself.

'I don't condone lies, but I can understand

your reasoning and overlook the falsehood because you are a woman and can't help yourself.
A beautiful, incredibly sensual woman...' he
said with a smile. 'I also realise why you were
so cranky at dinner. You dressed to flirt because
you were feeling neglected all day.' He was so
sure of himself he didn't try to cover his arrogance.

'You are unbelievable.' Selina stared at Rion in
a kind of fascinated horror. His reasoning was so
wrong it was almost funny. She wondered what
he would say if she told him the truth—that she
still loved him and her behaviour had been a defence mechanism to hide the fact.

'What did you want me to do after your little
act?' The smile left his face. 'Change my schedule? Demand to know who the Arab sheikh was?
You know me, Selina. Who I am...what I do.
And what I never do is jealousy.'

'You could have fooled me,' she shot back furiously. 'Answering my phone with your macho
posturing—you have put me in the impossible
position where I will have to lie to Beth yet again

and invent a man friend. Sometimes you make me sick, Rion. Do you ever think of anyone but yourself?'

'Well, I am thinking of you right now,' he drawled mockingly, his hand moving from her shoulder around the nape of her neck.

Selina lost it. She pummelled him on the chest. 'Sex is not thinking of another person,' she flung at him, her amber eyes flaring wildly. 'For you it is simply what you want and get with no thought for anyone else.' She saw the blaze of fury in his night-black eyes and didn't care. 'Well, tough— it is not on the agenda tonight.' She was shaking with temper and staggered back a few steps, moisture hazing her vision, her emotions haywire. 'Get out, Rion. Just get out…'

Rion saw the shimmer of tears in Selina's eyes and the black anger he felt at her tirade faded a little. She was upset, emotional, and he was useless at dealing with emotional women. He didn't do emotions.

'Don't worry, I'm going. A hysterical woman

and knowing I am your dirty little secret is a bit of a turn off. I'll see you in the morning,' he said bluntly and left, closing the door behind him.

CHAPTER NINE

'THIS is ridiculous, Rion. I don't like shopping and I don't need a new dress. I'd rather stay on board.'

It was three-thirty in the afternoon; the yacht was docked in the Grand Harbour of Malta. Rion was wearing an immaculate silver-grey suit, white shirt and striped tie, every magnificent inch of him screaming dynamic, wealthy and powerful male. Selina, wearing her white linen pants and a shirt, was glaring defiantly up at him.

'I beg to differ. Nice as they are, the only three dresses you appear to possess—the yellow, blue and black—are not suitable for the dinner party tonight. Justin and his wife will expect the best. You need something glamorous—and not black. Spend what you like, and get shoes, jewellery—

whatever it takes. Now, get in the car, or I will be late for my meeting. The chauffeur will drop me off, then ferry you around the shops and return you to the yacht.'

'Right—fine.' She leapt into the backseat of the car, insulted.

She was still smarting from last night, and the telephone call she'd received from Beth at dawn this morning had not helped. Beth had wanted to know who the man was. Trevor had told her he sounded quite commanding and jealous, and Beth had asked for the whole story of her holiday romance and if he was a keeper...

Lying to her friend, she'd told her it was another passenger—a widower who was holidaying on his own, with whom she had struck up a friendship, just a friendship, and was enjoying his company. Whether Beth had believed her or not she wasn't sure, but she'd changed the subject to work and ended the call.

Rion slid in beside her, his arm along the back of the seat, his thigh brushing Selina's, making her body instantly aware of him. And that infuriated her even more. She would spend his money and enjoy doing it, she decided. She could donate the lot to charity, she thought, when they got to Greece in two more days.

All of a sudden the thought was not so satisfying…

Rion wanted glamorous—and, taking a last look at her reflection in the mirror, Selina grinned. The hairdresser had done wonders, and glamour was what he was getting—in spades. She left the cabin.

The silk crepe dress in midnight-blue had cost a fortune, as had the shoes that she had teamed with it—so much that her conscience had got the better of her and she had refrained from buying the jewellery Rion had casually suggested.

Rion heard Dimitri gasp and turned his head. He did a double take as Selina walked towards him.

'Is this glamorous enough for you?' she asked.

Rion was speechless. This was a Selina he had never seen before. Her gorgeous hair was swept up in a crown of curls on top of her head, a few strands of curls left to fall artfully either side of her beautiful face. Her huge amber eyes were cleverly accentuated by the use of eyeshadow and mascara, her lush lips painted a deep scarlet. Her make-up was subtle but perfect.

As for the dress she wore—no wonder Dimitri had gasped. It left little to the imagination. Jewel-encrusted straps over her shoulders widened into two triangular pieces of material that just about covered her breasts and tucked into a tight band beneath. The skirt hugged her hips and thighs to end a couple of inches above her knees. She was wearing sheer silk stockings and on her feet were jewelled shoes with killer heels.

'You look exquisite—if a little daring,' Rion drawled, eyeing her breasts, and looped an arm around her waist. He spun her around. The straps over her shoulders curved under her arms and left her back bare almost to the base of her spine, where a concealed zip held the fabric taut across her rear.

She shot him a glance over her shoulder. 'Great, isn't it?' A feline glitter was in her amber eyes.

'You can't wear that!' He grasped her arm and spun her back to face him. She looked spectacular in the dress and she knew it—but it was for his eyes only... 'One spectacular cleavage is enough. You are almost showing two. Change to the black.'

Captain Ted walked in. 'The car has arrived on the dock. Your guests are getting—' He stopped, his eyes widening on Selina.

'Right—we are coming,' Rion said, and moved his hand from her arm to splay it across her back. He bent his head towards her as he led her outside. 'Too late now to change, but be warned: I really missed you last night, and two can play your game,' he murmured huskily, and let his fingers trail down her spine. He felt her quiver.

That Rion had admitted he had missed her shocked Selina into silence.

And she was having second thoughts about the dress as they stood at the top of the gangway to welcome their guests. Held close to Rion's side, with his hand caressing her back, was a kind of torture and her breath hitched in her throat. She shot him a sidelong glance. 'Stop it,' she hissed.

'Sexual attraction works both ways—painful, isn't it?' He grinned and straightened up. 'Our guests have arrived.' And thankfully for Selina his hand slid from her back and he took a step forward.

Her body still heated from his seductive touch. She glanced at the couple who had joined them on deck and then looked again, her amber eyes widening in horror. She froze, the blood turning to ice in her veins.

Selina concentrated on the woman. She was in her mid-forties, and very elegantly dressed. But all the time her mind was spinning, hoping she was wrong about the man…

She heard the man introduce his wife to Rion. Then Rion slipped his arm around her waist again, his fingers pressing her side, but she did not so much as flinch.

'Selina, this is Justin Bratchet and his wife, Alice.'

Numb with shock, Selina shook hands with Alice first and tried to smile, spouting the social niceties, until finally she had no choice but to look at the man—Justin Bratchet.

She felt her flesh crawl as she shook hands with him, and forced a smile to her lips. 'Nice to meet you,' she lied, and pulled her hand free with indecent haste.

The dinner was informative, but also a living nightmare as far as Selina was concerned—from which she escaped as fast as she could.

Rion saw the couple ashore at the end of the evening and walked back on board. The evening had been a success, his meeting earlier had gone well, and the deal—after a bit of adjustment— looked like being a cinch. Though Selina's behaviour had been a bit odd. He had sensed her tense the minute she'd met the couple, and he'd seen the look in her eyes as he introduced her to Justin. He had a gut feeling she knew the man. And she had excused herself from seeing the couple off the yacht with the plea that she needed the bathroom, which was odd.

Maybe Selina had bumped into Bratchet on her travels? This morning Rion had searched Selina's name on the internet—something he had never done before. She'd taken some finding, but he'd been surprised at what he'd discovered. She was listed as a translator for a top international agency noted for its discretion and hired by governments and the like. There was a shot of her looking stunning but businesslike, standing at the side of an Arab sheikh at an international trade fair in China. Other delegates included a few heads of state. Selina was obviously at the top of her career ladder and had to be making a very comfortable living. Maybe he was wrong about her and she *wasn't* a typical gold-digging female...

Reaching his cabin, he opened the door and saw at a glance she wasn't there. Kicking off his shoes, he removed his jacket and tie and dropped them on the bed, flicking open the buttons of his shirt. He walked next door, contemplating removing that incredible gown with a smile on his face which broadened when he saw the view of Selina's slender back. She had removed her shoes and was minus her stockings—lace-trimmed, he noted. Pity. He had wanted to peel them off.

His sensual smile vanished when he realised she was talking on her phone and that was the reason for her hasty retreat.

The click of the door opening alerted Selina, and abruptly she ended the conversation and rang off. She turned around. 'Oh, it's you,' she said inanely.

Rion gazed straight back at her from below thick, curling lashes, his expression bland. 'Obviously. Who did you want it to be? The man on the phone?' he queried, and in two lithe strides he was towering over her.

'It wasn't a man—it was Aunt Peggy,' Selina said, but could not look him in the eyes.

'You called her at twelve at night?' he

prompted, and tipped up her chin with one long finger so she had no choice but to look at him.

'Yes,' she said thinking fast. 'It is a little earlier in England.'

Rion raised a brow, dark eyes gleaming with suspicion. 'I'll believe you—but what else might I have got wrong, I wonder? I had the distinct feeling you had met Justin Bratchet before tonight. Have you?'

Shaking her head, she dislodged his finger and taking a step back, gave an emphatic 'No!' relieved she could tell the truth.

'Yet you seemed to recognise him. Maybe from your travels? I looked you up on Google today and discovered you really are a high-flyer in your profession.'

'You did what?'

'You are listed on the website of the international agency you work for.'

'Oh.' She was glad she'd had the foresight to tell Beth not to list her on the charity's website. She valued her career, and at least one of her previous employers would not be happy discovering what she did in her spare time. 'Anyway, I don't know and have never met Mr Bratchet before, and with luck I will never meet him again,' she said adamantly.

'You could have fooled me. I have met the man a few times in New York and I know he has a reputation of being a bit of a womaniser. You seemed to be encouraging him.'

She had, because she'd wanted to find out where he was going, and had succeeded. But she couldn't tell Rion that.

'When he asked you what you did you responded flightily—"As little as possible." Which I know is a lie. Why?'

'Because it is easier to tell that type of rich man who thinks he is God what he wants to hear—satisfied?' she snapped. She had said more than she ought. Plus Rion, barefoot and with his shirt undone, was an endearing sight.

'You really have it in for the poor man,' Rion returned, studying her flushed face. 'So he likes women and flirts? Hardly an offence.'

'Yes, well, you would say that—given he is

your friend. It is his wife I feel sorry for, poor woman.'

'Your sympathy is wasted on Alice. She was a widow when she married Justin three years ago. He takes care of her and her daughter, and now her grandson. She has hit the jackpot; trust me, she will never leave him. I recognised the type the minute I met her.'

'Okay—if you say so,' she agreed. It was late and this conversation was going nowhere.

'Is that another example of telling a man what he wants to hear?' Rion asked sardonically and reached for her shoulders to draw her close. 'Not that I mind in this instance,' he mocked, and kissed her with a hungry thoroughness that left her breathless.

He pulled the shoulder straps of her dress down her arms and she helped, wanting to block the horrible evening from her mind and craving what she knew only Rion could give her. She gazed up into his lustrous dark eyes, shaded with passion, and her heart raced.

'I knew you were braless,' Rion groaned. 'You

have perfect breasts,' he murmured, his dark gaze lingering on the creamy mounds for a moment before he lifted his eyes to hers. 'You have no idea what you do to me, Selina. I have been aching to remove this dress from the second I saw you wearing it.'

'I thought it would appeal to you,' she replied.

Rion smiled and began removing his clothes. Breathless, she simply stared as he revealed his magnificent bronzed body to her avid gaze, and she reached for the dress at her waist, eager to wriggle out of it.

'No, let me,' Rion commanded. He picked her up and laid her down on the bed and stretched out beside her. 'I want to take it off.'

He folded an arm around her and she was suddenly on her stomach. He trailed a string of kisses down her spine and slowly peeled her dress over her hips. Her whole body trembled as his clever fingers stroked and caressed while his lips continued their devastating path down her thighs, the backs of her knees. With the dress finally removed he turned her over and kissed and caressed his way back up her body. Finally his mouth took hers in a deeply passionate kiss as he settled between her thighs.

Selina wrapped her arms around him as if he was the only solid matter in the universe, her hands caressing his satin-smooth skin, tracing the length of his spine as she planted frantic kisses on the broad chest, the dark male nipples. She heard his guttural growl as, lifting her hips, he surged into her willing body, and she cried out with the exquisite pleasure of his possession, the feeling intensifying with every powerful thrust, growing into a mindless, mutually ecstatic climax.

But later—much later—listening to the steady sound of Rion's breathing, she realised that tonight even the oblivion of orgasmic sex was not going to help her sleep.

Luckily she had never told Rion about the rescue centre Beth and her husband ran in Cambodia for a children's charity. Selina had helped to set it up and finance it.

She and Beth had spent their last summer

vacation before finishing university travelling through Thailand and Cambodia. Beth had met Trevor, an American, and it had been love at first sight. It was Trevor who had shown them the horrific child sex trade in Cambodia and explained how unscrupulous dealers travelled the countryside, telling poor families who lived off the land that they had a job for their son or daughter in a big city hotel, as a maid or boot boy, and offering them money. Of course there was no hotel work—though the children were kept in a hotel of sorts, where they were abused and forced into the sex trade. The really tragic part for Selina was that the children, after having to suffer such vile abuse from adults every day of their young lives, were too ashamed to tell their parents what was really happening to them.

Planeloads of men flew into the capital regularly from Europe, Japan and the USA, on specially organised sex trips. A lot of them wanted children—the younger the better.

Trevor had explained that the reason he knew

so much about the trade was because his father worked for the American government,
and the USA was one of the few countries to
have passed a law enabling them to extradite
any American citizen arrested for paedophilia
in Cambodia and take them back to the USA
to stand trial. The sentences there were a lot
harsher. It had been listening to his father talk
about his work and seeing the damage done for
himself that had made Trevor determined to set
up a rescue centre.

Beth, always passionate about injustice, was
his perfect partner, and during that holiday the
idea for a rescue charity was born. Selina had
never touched her divorce settlement because
she'd still had her father's trust fund. She'd left
university the following summer and donated
the money to help set up the charity. With the
help of Beth's father the legal technicalities had
been dealt with, and property bought. It had
been converted into a fifteen-bedroomed centre with schoolrooms, craft rooms—everything

necessary to help the children to regain their self worth and equip them with the skills to earn a legitimate living.

Beth and Trevor had got married at Christmas. Selina had been a bridesmaid. The following year, the rescue centre had opened, and with the help of a Cambodian politician, a police inspector and a local lawyer, they'd taken in ten children. Selina had stayed for three months to help, then spent the next three months in Australia, working as a translator for a tourist firm on the Gold Coast that specialised in Chinese tourists, and taking her diving certificate in her spare time. Then she had signed on with the international agency she still worked with now.

To date the centre had rescued over forty children—some of them as young as six. All had been counselled and some had returned to their families. Some had learnt new skills and found legitimate work, others were still at the centre, and sadly a couple of the older girls—if you could call fourteen old—had gone back to the sex trade. They were already HIV-positive and sure that in their culture no man was ever going to marry them…

Accepting a glass of fresh orange juice from Louis, Selina refused any food. Cradling the glass in her hand, she crossed to the huge glass doors that opened out onto the deck and paused for a moment. The sun was hot in a cloudless sky, as it had been for the whole trip—which was now almost over. She felt her heart contract with the knowledge.

Rion was seated at the table, wearing the familiar khaki shorts. His tanned shoulders were slightly hunched as he forked scrambled egg into his mouth with one hand, his other tapping something into a laptop.

One more night with him and it would be over. They would reach Greece tomorrow, conclude their business deal and cut the last slender link that bound them. Never to meet again. She would have her inheritance—or to be precise, Anna and the Taylor Foundation would. A satisfactory outcome, she told herself. Rion would move on to another woman, and she…well, she would what?

'Don't just stand there—come and join me.'

Selina didn't answer her own question. She looked at Rion's smiling face and walked across to take the seat opposite. 'You looked occupied,' she said, glancing at his laptop and then up at him. 'Do you ever stop working?' she asked, and took a sip of her orange juice.

He reached across and took her free hand in his. Raising it to his mouth, he kissed her palm, sending an electric sensation up her arm. A knowing, intimate smile curved his lips as she eased her hand from his.

'I am going to in about half an hour. I have a few things to check out on the Bratchet deal—it is looking good, if a little expensive.'

'You are going into business with that man?' she asked, carefully placing her glass on the table.

'No—not into business *with* him.' The relief she felt was quickly destroyed as Rion continued, 'He wants to sell up and has offered me first refusal on buying him out. It is a good deal—not so much for the motor trade he runs but for the prime location of the property he owns in New York. Even in a recession you can never lose on owning land in one of the greatest cities in the world. Bratchet knows that, and I am surprised he wants to sell simply because he has finally married and wants to play happy families with Alice and his stepchildren. He is asking more than I want to pay, but everything in life is negotiable and I'll get it for the right price in the end.' He grinned.

'Yes,' Selina agreed numbly. The irony did not escape her that the only time Rion had ever discussed his work with her was now. She had a good idea why Bratchet was selling up. And she could not bear to think why he doted on his step-grandson…

'Give me five minutes, and you will have my undivided attention for the rest of the day.'

'Okay.' She watched Rion turn back to his laptop and, deep in thought, sipped at her orange juice, oblivious to the beauty of the day.

The day before the opening of the rescue centre in Cambodia she had been sitting talking with Trevor's father, Clint, in the foyer of his hotel. He had pointed Justin Bratchet out to her as the man walked across to the reception desk to check out. Bratchet was a regular visitor to Cambodia to indulge his preference for young boys, he'd told her. A police contact had told Clint just that morning that Bratchet had finally been arrested the day before, because an eight-year-old boy he had abused had ended up in hospital. But Bratchet was a very wealthy man and had obviously bribed the right people. The charges had been dropped.

Selina had been horrified, and asked why the Americans didn't arrest him. Dryly Clint had told her they could not. They could only extradite the man to stand trial at home if the Cambodian authorities arrested him first, but they would get him eventually, Clint had said. Bratchet might have got a fright and would stay away for a while, but he would be back. His sort couldn't help themselves.

At dinner last night Selina had managed to discover that Bratchet was going to the Far East on business the next day, while his wife was going back to America.

'Right, Selina, no more work. How would you like to go scuba-diving off Gozo today?'

She swallowed the *yes* that rose in her throat and let her eyes rest on Rion. 'I thought we were sailing for Greece this morning?'

'I'm not in any rush. We can take a day or two longer if you like.'

If he had said that yesterday she might have agreed, but not now... Last night her call had not been to her Aunt Peggy but to Trevor. A quick call, to tell him she had seen Bratchet dining in Malta with his wife and learned that Bratchet was leaving tomorrow for the Far East without his wife. Maybe he was tired of matrimony. She'd told him to look out for the man and rung off with the excuse that her new friend was waiting for her—which, in a way, had been true...

'What about your business deal with Bratchet? You said it was expensive—are you still going to pursue it?' She wanted Rion to say no.

'Of course I am. What have you got against the man? The fact he flirted with you?'

'No, I am far too mature for him anyway,' Selina said, with a dry irony that was lost on Rion. 'I just think there is something a bit sleazy about him.' She wanted to tell Rion the truth, but she wasn't sure she could trust him.

Rion got to his feet and came round to her. Taking her hand in his, he drew her up. He looked down into her lovely but serious face.

'When a good deal is to be made the man offering it could be a serial killer for all I care. As long as it is legitimate, business is business.' He should have known better than to try and talk business with a woman. 'Now, do you want to go to Gozo or not?'

'Not,' Selina said, resignation filling her, and, pulling her hands from his, she took a step back. There was no future for them anyway—why prolong the agony by another day?

After what Rion had said she knew she could not tell him about Bratchet. She had trusted Rion once with her heart and he had broken it. Much as she still loved him she did not dare trust him again—not when other people, children, were involved.

If her hunch was right and Bratchet was on his way to Cambodia she knew Rion well enough to know he would tell the man. Maybe not in the pursuit of business, but out of genuine disgust at what the man was. But either way Bratchet would be warned.

'We had a deal, you and I. Two weeks—and it ends tomorrow back in Greece. I sign the shares over to you, you pay me, and that's the end.'

She glanced up. His tanned perfectly carved features were set in a cold mask. The flicker of pain she thought she'd seen in his dark eyes must have been a figment of her imagination, she dismissed a second later.

'You are right, Selina. A deal is a deal. But it is not quite that simple,' he said in a cold, flat tone. 'I'll tell Ted to prepare to leave immediately, and arrange with Kadiekis to meet us when we dock with the relevant documents. I spoke to him the day after we left Letos and he agreed to inform Anna by letter according to the terms you and I worked out for her. She has probably received the notification by now so there should be no problem.' And, turning, he walked away.

'Wait.' She looked around, feeling guilty she had not thought to ask Rion about the lawyer. 'You have left your laptop,' she said weakly. He turned, his gaze flicking over her scathingly. 'The heat will damage it...' She trailed off as in a few lithe strides he picked up the laptop from the table and stopped in front of her.

'Such concern for my property is admirable, Selina, and as *you* also belong to me for another day,' he reminded her, with a predatory smile that left her in no doubt what he meant, 'I'll see you later.'

A deep, brooding frown creased Rion's brow as he stood on the bridge as the yacht left the harbour. He knew women, and knew Selina had enjoyed the trip as much as he had, but she had turned down his offer to extend the cruise flat. She could not wait a minute longer than she had to to get away, and it bothered him.

He should be content. He had done what he had planned to do—have a relaxing break made all the more satisfying by Selina. He had got his revenge for her betrayal and enjoyed every minute. He was ready to get back to work full-time—especially with the Bratchet deal.

So why wasn't he satisfied? And why did *Selina* and *revenge* in the same sentence make him feel thoroughly ashamed of himself?

CHAPTER TEN

'Sɪᴛ.' Rion indicated a chair in front of his desk and walked around to take the seat behind it. He let his eyes rest coolly on Selina.

She was wearing the black dress she had worn for her grandfather's funeral. Her hair was pulled back into a single thick plait to hang down her back, her face was carefully made up, and high-heeled shoes were on her dainty feet. He watched her smooth the skirt of the dress over her hips and thighs as she sat down, placing the black satchel she carried on her lap. She looked elegant and businesslike, but in his mind's eye he was picturing her gorgeous body naked—her soft skin, the perfect breasts he had tasted so many times. Only last night she had been like a living flame in his arms. They had made love well into the early hours of the morning. Yet now she sat there, seemingly cool and composed, wanting the money...

Selina glanced around the huge office—all glass and steel, hard like the man. They'd met the lawyer over breakfast and pretended they were good friends while Kadiekis explained the handing over of her grandfather's shares to her so she could sell them to Rion before the estate was finally wound up. That way the provision they had agreed for Anna was guaranteed and all debts would be covered. There would still be a healthy amount of money left over for Selina. She had signed the paper he'd given her, confirming the fact, and another notified document to cancel the guardianship. That had been fraught enough. Especially when he'd given the share certificates straight to Rion for safekeeping, as though she was some silly woman who would lose them before she got ashore.

But the trip from the marina in a chauffeured car to Rion's office in Athens had taken almost an hour, and been a whole lot worse.

Rion had worked on his laptop or made calls

the whole time, never saying a word to her. Not that she had wanted him to, but sitting beside him in the close confines of the car with the slight scent of his cologne tantalising her nostrils, she had been intensely aware of him. Wearing an immaculate grey suit, with his black hair swept back from his brow, he'd looked broodingly attractive, and she hadn't been able to help noting every tiny movement he made—his arm touching hers when he raised the phone to his ear, the deep velvet tone of his voice, the accidental brush of his thigh against hers with the movement of the vehicle.

By the time she'd got out of the car she'd been hot, tense, her nerves wound tight as a drum. And her nervous tension had not improved when he'd taken her arm and led her into what was obviously a new building—nothing like the old office she had visited once when they were married. Then he'd urged her into the elevator, and now had ordered her to 'Sit.'

'I am not a dog,' she said tartly, to break the growing silence.

'No,' he said, and lifted a black brow.

The insult, not spoken but implied, enraged her. This was the man she had stupidly, eagerly given her body to last night—and her heart and soul, if she was honest, because she'd known it would be the final time.

'Trading insults is your thing, Rion. Why am I not surprised?' she sneered. 'You traded me once for a company, and again for sex. You'd trade with the devil himself—Bratchet for one. Now, give me the form to sign. Why we could not have done this on the yacht I will never understand. Then let me get out of here.'

'You are overreacting to an imagined insult. And let's get one thing straight,' he said curtly. 'I would never have married you to acquire the Stakis shipping line. I married you because I'd had unprotected sex with you. With the possibility you might be pregnant it seemed the right thing to do at the time.'

Appalled, Selina stared at him, the air between them crackling with tension. 'My God—and that is supposed to make me feel better? Just give me the damn paper to sign.'

Not a muscle moved in Rion's face as he pushed the relevant documents across the desk. He was within a hair's breadth of losing his temper with her, but with a terrific effort of will he controlled the urge to shake some sense into her. She wanted him. He wanted her. But she blew hot and cold for no apparent reason and arguing with her would get him nowhere. The day wasn't over yet, and with business out of the way he had plans to end it with Selina in his bed.

'This is a copy of the official notification from Kadiekis agreeing to the sale of your grandfather's shares to me before the estate is wound up. You'd better keep that. And these are the share certificates, which you might like to check to make sure they add up to what I told you. Finally, a transferral form, which you should read and sign where indicated.'

'I don't need to read it. Just give me a pen.'

'Is that wise? How do you know you can trust me?' he asked with a cynical arch of an ebony brow. 'From what you just said, you don't have much of an opinion of me.'

Mr Cool, Selina thought—while she was getting madder by the minute. 'No, I don't. At least not on a normal human level. But when it comes to a deal I know you are meticulous to the nth degree,' she mocked. And, picking up the pen he had pushed across the desk, she signed the document. Standing up, she handed it to him. Then, placing the copy of the agreement he had suggested she keep in her satchel, she took out a notepad and wrote down her bank account number. Tearing it off, she held the page out to Rion.

'You will need this. When you and Kadiekis have settled everything I would like any money that is left transferred to this account. That way we need never communicate again.' The quicker she got out of here the better. She was perilously close to losing her temper altogether and telling Rion exactly what she thought of him. She might love him, but as a man he was a waste of space…

Rion's eyes narrowed sardonically on her beautiful face. 'I do have to sign as well, Selina.' He knew she was hiding something. Her mention of Bratchet and the devil in the same sentence had set him thinking, and he was determined to find out what it was. Taking the document, he signed it. 'Did you notice how much money you will receive?' he asked, hoping to delay her. Taking the note from her hand, he felt her flinch as their fingers touched.

'What you said a fortnight ago, I presume.'

'Yes, that is correct.' Glancing at the number on the note he wrote something else on it and turned to the computer on his desk. 'I'll enter your account number in the relevant file, and I might as well arrange the transfer of the shares now with my broker.'

In a matter of minutes it was done. Then, rising to his feet he walked around the desk and handed the note back to her.

'In the unlikely event that anything goes wrong and you need to contact me, my personal cell phone number is on there.' She took it, avoiding touching him this time, he noted. 'Have you thought what you are going to do with the money that is left?' he asked, wanting to delay her departure. He saw relief mingled with the anger in her expressive eyes.

'Give it to a children's charity,' she said, pushing the note into her handbag and slinging it over her shoulder. 'Now I'll be on my way.'

'The same children's charity as before, I presume?' he prompted, not convinced by her glib reply any more than he had been the first time.

'Yes.' She turned to go.

'Not so fast.' He wrapped his hand around her upper arm and spun her back to face him. 'You and I are not finished yet.'

Selina glanced at Rion, furious at his bullying tactic to delay her. She had had enough. 'We were finished years ago.' She tried to pull her arm free but he simply tightened his grip, his fingers digging into her flesh, and she lost her temper completely. 'My God, Iris did me a favour, telling me about you.'

'Iris?' He looked puzzled. 'Telling you what?'

'You are supposed to be brilliant—work it out,' she snapped.

His other hand slid up her back to catch her long silken plait and tug her head back. 'Cut out the sarcasm and tell me.'

Held in his firm grip, Rion's eyes boring down into hers, she registered the implacable determination in the dark depths. Refusing to be intimidated, she thought, why not? Their business was concluded, and Rion could do with being taken down a peg or two.

'It wasn't my grandfather who told me about the marriage deal, as you seem to think. It was your half sister, Iris.'

'Iris? I don't believe you. She did not know.'

'Yes, she did. She heard her parents talking in the car on the way back from our engagement party. How ironic is that?' She felt him stiffen, his hand falling from her hair—though he still kept hold of her arm. Shaking her head, she eyed him contemptuously. 'And she told me a lot more. The day you threw me out you told her never to speak to me again, but she did. Jason was *her* boyfriend. Iris had told him to follow her up to her bedroom—right at the top of the stairs. But he was drunk. He turned left and passed out in my bed. I never knew he was there because I'd gone to bed early with a couple of strong painkillers.'

Selina was on a roll. Everything Rion had denied her the right to tell him came spilling out with a vengeance.

'Iris knew the truth. Jason told her he'd heard a noise in the hall, woken up. He saw red hair on the pillow and realised his mistake. Horrified, he dashed out of the bedroom. I begged her to tell you, but she was too frightened of what her bossy older brother would do. Knowing you, I can't say I blame her—and in fact, as it turned out it was lucky for me. She told me about the marriage deal and what a womaniser you are. Who did you think showed me the shots of you and your lady friends on the computer? I didn't have one at the time. Who do you think told me the woman you really loved and wanted to marry was Lydia, but she married someone else?'

Shocked rigid, Rion stared down into angry golden eyes glinting with shards of green and knew she was telling the truth. The story was so bizarre it had to be true. That Iris, his half-sister whom he had always protected, had been dating the boy and had known the truth all along and refused to tell him horrified him. All this time he had thought Selina had betrayed him, and she hadn't…

A great wide chasm opened up in his mind, filled with memories he had banked down for years. The innocence Selina had gifted him, their wedding day when he had watched her walk down the aisle and thought her the most beautiful bride he had ever seen, the love she had given him unconditionally and he had taken for granted. How could he have been so arrogant, so stiff-necked with pride as to throw her out? What did that make him? And he had taken one look at Selina on the beach at Letos the night before the funeral and wanted her so badly he had blackmailed her into his bed.

'Why didn't you—?'

'Tell you?' Selina jeered, cutting him off. 'You refused to see me, speak or listen to me, remember...?' She saw him flinch. He had a right to. He didn't like the truth. 'Then you had the audacity to try to name *me* as the adulterous party. What a joke, given your reputation. I told Beth what had happened and thanks to her and her dad I fought you and won. It was the best thing I ever did. Beth reckoned you got off lightly. I should have demanded more money. But it was enough for me to get my self-esteem back, and the whole affair taught me a lesson I will never forget.'

'What would that be?' Rion asked not sure he wanted to know the answer. But he wanted to keep her talking while his mind grappled with the enormity of what she had revealed. What had he done?

'To work hard, get a career and *never* count on a man to take care of me. With the shining examples of my biological father, my grandfather and my ex-husband I find it remarkably easy to remember,' she said sarcastically. 'Now, if you don't mind, I am leaving.' And, tightening her grip on her satchel, she pulled her arm free.

'No, not yet.' Thinking fast for a reason to make her stay, he said, 'I have not given you the salary you've lost for the last two weeks. I said I would.'

'Forget it. I have.'

'No. What I am trying to say is I owe you an apology, Selina—more than an apology. I don't expect you to forgive me for not trusting you when we were married, but you have to admit finding a half-naked man dashing out of our bedroom looked bad.'

Selina couldn't help it—she laughed…if a little hysterically. Rion could not be contrite in a million years. 'Even when you try to apologise you still have to qualify it with your opinion. You could have asked.' She put a finger on her chin and flashed him a pseudo-pensive glance. 'Oh, no, you couldn't. You wouldn't speak to me!'

His lips twisted. 'Cute, Selina. But please listen. I am serious. I have done you a terrible injustice—more than one.' Grasping her shoulders, he held her still. 'I want to make it up to you any way I can.'

She looked up and caught the grim urgency in his expression, the sincerity in the dark eyes that bored into hers—and the underlying gleam of awareness in the glittering depths. His great body was too close. She felt the pressure of his strong hands, the flexing of his long fingers on her arms, and knew she had to get out of here fast—before her traitorous body succumbed once again to the wonder of his.

'More money? Forget it.' She had to get away with her pride intact. It was all she had left.

'No…yes. I mean I will marry you again—have a home, children.' Rion was almost as shocked as Selina looked by what he'd said. Then like a lightning strike, electrifying in its intensity, it hit him. He actually meant every word…

During the time he had spent with Selina on the yacht he'd been more relaxed, more alive, and had more genuine fun than at any other time in his life. But it wasn't just sex. It had never been just sex with Selina, but love. He had made *love* to her, and been too blinkered, too arrogant to see it until now. He loved Selina…

Selina's lips parted in shock and for a moment her foolish heart leapt. Then reality clicked in. Nothing had changed. Rion didn't love her.

'Marry you again…? Are you mad…?'

She recognised his proposal for what it was. For once in his life the great Orion Moralis was feeling guilty. Well, he could drown in that for all she cared. He had made her feel guilty even when she had done nothing wrong. If he thought he could salve his conscience by marrying her again he was in for a big surprise. She was amazed he had the cheek to ask. In fact she was insulted and, feeling about him as she did, it hurt. And he had hurt her enough already to last a lifetime…

'As for a home and children—you have to be joking. I don't like the company you keep.'

'A simple no would have sufficed. And what the hell do you mean by "the company I keep"?' Rion demanded, his grip tightening.

For an instant she felt afraid. But she refused to be intimidated by a man—any man...

'Bratchet for one,' she sneered. Rion led a gilded life, and it was time he learnt not everyone was so fortunate. 'I know you didn't believe me, but I *did* give your money to a children's charity. A charity that is needed because of depraved perverts like him, who put a boy of eight in hospital. It made my flesh crawl to shake his hand.'

She looked Rion straight in the eyes and told him about the charity Beth and Trevor ran, of which she was a silent partner and one of the main supporters. She felt him tense but spared him nothing, telling him the painfully tragic details with all the passion of a caring woman committed to the cause.

Rion let his hands fall from Selina's shoulders. He could not believe what he was hearing. Of course he had heard as much as any normal person about the trade in child sex, but as he listened to her with growing horror his face paled. He was appalled at what she told him, and appalled at how badly he had misjudged her and how spectacularly he had failed to protect the innocent girl he had married from ever having to come into contact with such a sick, depraved side of life.

'I had no idea,' he murmured.

'Why would you? In your world business and money is God,' she said flatly. 'Though you would be surprised how many very wealthy men like Bratchet use and abuse children. Perversion cuts across all levels of society and it costs money to fly to Cambodia,' she opined cynically.

'And you compare *me* with Bratchet?' Rion queried hollowly.

'No.' She knew Rion's sexual preferences all too well. Seeing him standing there watching her with dark haunted eyes, she felt her heart swell with love and compassion and knew it was time to go. 'But people are usually judged by the company they keep, and as you said yourself yesterday, you would do business with a serial killer if it was legitimate and a good deal.'

Now Rion knew what she had been hiding—why she had refused to go on the dive. And, worse, he realised that one exaggerated throw-away comment he had made had killed any hope he had of keeping Selina.

'I know it is a lot to ask, because it is your precious business, but do me a favour when you speak to Bratchet again: don't mention what I have told you. When you caught me on the phone the other night I wasn't calling Aunt Peggy, but Trevor, to tell him I'd seen Bratchet and learnt he was heading back to the Far East. His sort never change, and with luck he might be caught and not be able to buy his way out again.'

'You have my word,' Rion promised quietly, but inside he was a seething mass of emotions—fury at Bratchet, and at himself for being so blind, so arrogant he had refused to recognise the love he felt for Selina until now, when she was leaving him.

'Thank you. And, hey, look on the bright side. If Bratchet *is* arrested you might get his company even cheaper and we'll both win,' she said facetiously.

Rion slowly shook his head, the hint of a smile quirking the corners of his mouth. 'You are an incredible lady, Selina.' Sadly he resigned himself to the fact she was never going to be his. He didn't deserve her after all he had done. 'I'll arrange you a flight back to England.'

'No need. I have already got my flights booked for Cambodia. I usually spend a month every year helping Beth and Trevor—though it is only going to be three weeks this time.'

Her eyes lifted to his and Rion saw the disdain in their amber depths. He knew she was remembering why her trip had been cut short. As was he. And if it was possible to feel worse he did.

'Then let me make a donation to the charity,' he offered.

'It is simple. Just mail the Taylor Foundation.' Selina reeled off the e-mail address. 'But I would make it anonymous. Beth is a real crusader for justice—much more high-minded than me.'

Rion didn't try to stop her when she turned to leave. Didn't even touch her. He didn't dare.

'Your luggage is in the car. I'll tell the chauffeur to take you where you want to go.'

His original thought of persuading Selina to stay a night or two more with him, never mind marry him, was dead in the water and, moving to sit at his desk, he simply nodded as she walked out of the door.

Half an hour later Rion hadn't moved, but still sat with his head in his hands. He knew with gut-wrenching certainty that the same day he had finally realised he loved Selina he had lost her...

The phone rang and he ignored it. His secretary walked in and he told her he was not to be disturbed for the rest of the day.

He glanced around his state-of-the-art office and rose to his feet to walk to the vast glass wall. He gazed out over Athens but it did nothing for him. He had health, wealth, work he enjoyed— a great life by any standard. Yet the one person he needed was forever unobtainable to him, and the pain was crippling.

CHAPTER ELEVEN

SELINA stopped in the centre of the elegant foyer of the luxurious hotel in the centre of Rio that had been her home for the past ten days and turned to smile up at Antonio. Six foot tall, powerfully built and wearing a black tuxedo, white dress shirt and red bow tie, he was strikingly attractive—and a refreshingly honest man for all his wealth.

'Thank you, Antonio, it was a lovely evening,' she said. 'And it has been a real pleasure working for you again. But I am leaving early in the morning so I will say goodbye now.' She held out her hand but, ignoring it, he caught her shoulders and kissed her on both cheeks.

'You could change your mind and accept my offer to stay on as my mistress,' he prompted with a grin. 'Currently I have a vacancy—in fact I will always have a vacancy for you, Selina.'

Stepping back, Selina laughed up at him, shaking her head. 'You are incorrigible, Antonio—and, no, I could not. But if you ever need a translator again you know how to find me.'

'True. And if you ever change your mind, Selina, or need me for anything you have my number. Call me. If I can't have you as a lover I'll settle for a friend.' He smiled.

Selina saw the warmth in his dark eyes and was touched. 'Thank you. I will. Goodbye.' And, turning on her heel, she headed for the bank of elevators without looking back.

Once in her room, she gave a sigh of contentment as she closed the door. Another successful job completed, she thought and, kicking off her shoes, crossed to sit on the edge of the king-sized bed. She began unpinning her hair from its intricate chignon.

Antonio Soares, the head of the largest mining consortium in Brazil and with interests worldwide, was one of the good guys, Selina reflected. She had met him two months ago, as a client in Australia, and she had travelled to China with him. Then he had hired her again for a Chinese delegation visit to Brazil. The trip had been a success for both parties, and tonight had been the final celebratory dinner before the delegation left in the morning.

She finger-combed her hair, smiling. Antonio was a self-confessed womaniser but he was also fun, and he made her laugh with tales of the doyennes of Brazilian society who kept trying to get him to marry their daughters. He was like Rion in a way—he worked hard and played hard—but, unlike Rion, Antonio was not hard of heart. She had met his ten-year-old son, Eduardo, and knew his much-loved wife had died in childbirth and he had no intention of ever replacing her.

In fact, she thought, given a year or so to get over Rion she might even accept Antonio's offer to be his mistress…

Rising to her feet, she reached around to untie the halter neck of her dress and paused. For the first time in the three months since leaving Rion she realised she was beginning to think more positively of the future, even considering another man. That had to be a sign she was getting better.

She was about to unfasten the bow at the back of her neck when she heard a loud knock on the door.

Odd, she thought, it was after eleven, and she had not ordered anything from room service. She walked towards the door, not intending to open it until she'd asked who it was. But she never got the chance. The door opened and a man walked in, slamming the door behind him.

'You!' Selina exclaimed, her eyes widening in shock even as her traitorous heart leapt as she recognised Rion. His hair was longer and falling over his brow, she noted, and his usual sartorial elegance had slipped a little. The superbly tailored navy suit he wore no longer fitted so well. The jacket was loose across his chest and he looked leaner, his handsome features honed to an even more chiselled edge.

'What on earth are you doing here?' she asked, shocked rigid. Her insides were shaking. 'And how did you get in?' Stupid question. 'Never mind. Just get out or I will call the manager.' She didn't like the ferocious look on his face and suddenly she was afraid.

'Call away, but it won't do you any good. I own this hotel, I have a key, and I want to talk to you.'

'Own the hotel?' she parroted, a host of conflicting emotions flooding through her. 'But how did you know I was here?' she demanded.

Rion ran his hands through his hair. It was that or grabbing Selina, and he didn't trust himself to touch her after witnessing the scene between her and Antonio Soares in the foyer. But he could not take his eyes off her. Her glorious hair tumbled around her bare shoulders and the golden-brown shot satin dress she wore revealed a tempting cleavage. The satin slid sensuously over her shapely body to the floor. She looked beautiful and sexy and she was driving him out of his mind.

Rion shrugged his shoulders in an attempt to ease the fierce tension in his long body. 'I decided to look you up.'

'Look me up... Hunt me down, more like,'

Selina said, her voice rising incredulously. Her amber eyes flashed with temper, clashing with blazing black, but she was too angry to care. A few minutes ago she'd been congratulating herself on beginning to get over Rion, and now, like some evil genie, he'd popped back into her life.

'What the hell for?' She swore. 'It is almost midnight in Brazil—halfway round the world from where you live, for heaven's sake—and yet here you are. Are you crazy?' she demanded furiously.

Rion grabbed her around the waist and hauled her hard against him. For an instant desire flared between them, and savagely she tried to crush it. But too late. She registered his eyes, glittering with an almost manic light.

'Crazy, maybe—but it is you who have made me this way. And I'll hunt you down to the ends of the earth if that is what it takes to get you back. Because I can't stand the thought of you with someone else. Everything in me—everything I am—yearns for you,' he declared harshly.

This was a Rion she had never seen before. He was like a man possessed. 'You can't just hunt—'

But he carried on as though she had not spoken, and being held against his body was making her temperature rise.

'Do you think I haven't suffered the torment of the damned since we parted? Knowing the truth almost unmanned me. You were mine first, and I don't give a damn about any in between as long as you are mine last. As for Antonio Soares—I spoke to him downstairs and he won't bother you again.'

'Spoke to him? Bother me?' She was turning into a parrot. 'Antonio is a client—a *friend*, you Neanderthal,' she shot back furiously, and tried to wriggle free. But he tightened his grip and with one hand stroked up her back, tangling his fingers in her hair and forcing her to look up into his dark face.

'Where you are concerned I am. I can't help myself. I lied when I told you I didn't do jealous. I only need to see you smile at a man to be consumed by the green-eyed monster because I love you. I don't expect you to believe me but I do.'

Selina blinked. Had she heard right…? No, it was impossible. She glared at him belligerently. 'If this is another ploy to get me into bed you are wasting your time. Now, let me go.'

'No. Never again, Selina.' He lowered his head and kissed her with a possessive, seductive hunger that she fought to resist. But her traitorous body betrayed her and she felt her heart thud, the blood flow thicker in her veins. She raised her hands to push him away, but somehow her fingers involuntarily splayed across his broad chest and crept around his neck as she gave in to the sensual awareness Rion never failed to arouse in her and kissed him back.

Rion groaned and buried his face against her throat, inhaling the delicate scent of her skin. 'Forgive me.' He lifted his head. 'I swore I wouldn't do this, wouldn't touch you until we'd talked and I'd explained.' His anguished expression tore at Selina's heart. 'I know I don't deserve you, but I do love you, Selina.'

Loved her? Was it possible? She raised a hand to feel his brow and brushed back a stray lock of hair. 'Are you ill? Have you got a fever or something?' She didn't dare to believe in a penitent, loving Rion.

'Only a fever for you. When I think of how brutally I cut you out of my life, divorced you without a word, I'm appalled. Discovering that my own sister was too frightened of me to tell me the truth makes me cringe inside. I never considered myself a vengeful person, and yet I took advantage of your grandfather's will on the day of his funeral and used your generous heart, your caring for Anna, to get you back in my bed.'

'You're a ruthless man when you want something,' Selina said bluntly. Though her lips throbbed sensuously from his kiss, and his confession was balm to her wounded heart, she was still not prepared to believe the seismic change from outraged macho male to supplicant lover.

'I know. It is my character, I guess, but I am working to change it.'

A hint of a smile twitched Selina's lips.

'I can't help it—the same way I can't help wanting you. I love you, but I can't find the words to describe my feelings. I have never had to try before,' Rion said with a touch of his usual arrogance, pressing her closer to his long body.

The heat and the strength of him enveloped her.

'To say I love you sounds so tame in comparison to what I really feel. That last day in my office, when I realised you had never betrayed me and I asked you to marry me again, that was the moment I finally recognised the limitless depths of my feelings for you…that I loved you.'

Five times he had mentioned love, and Selina was beginning to believe him. 'You don't have to tell me this,' she said gently, noticing the lines of tiredness etched about his eyes, his mouth. Lifting a finger, she traced the contours of his lean, harshly handsome face. He was either ill or he did love her, and she knew which she'd prefer.

'Yes I do. For a few glorious moments I was euphoric. Then in less than a minute I was in hell. When you told me you didn't like the company I kept and why, and I realised what you did with your money...the Taylor Foundation... I had never been so horrified or ashamed in my whole life. Then I realised from your parting statement that I had in one careless comment made you forever associate me with that monster, Bratchet, and I had to let you walk away.'

'Oh, no...' She was shaken by the bleakness of his tone, and wanted to reassure him. 'You might be arrogant, and look and act like a ruthless tycoon sometimes—well, most of the time—but I would never ever compare you with that horrible man.'

'Thank you—I think,' he said wryly, and brushed his lips across hers in the briefest of kisses. 'That is what Dimitri said a week ago, when he arrived in Athens to visit his parents and we had a drink together. It is thanks to him I am here. He told me I looked a wreck, and asked me what had happened. I'd had a bit to drink and told him the story of our relationship. He told me I was a coward. If I loved you I had to fight for you. Then he mentioned he had seen you leaving an airport in Rio with Antonio Soares as he was dashing to catch a flight to Greece. He also told me there was a picture of you and Soares in some geological magazine, taken in China a month ago, and if I had a grain of sense I wouldn't waste any more time. Am I too late?'

Selina lifted wide amber eyes to his but his long lashes lowered, shielding his eyes. But they could not quite hide the unfamiliar vulnerability in their black depths.

'Or can I hope?'

'Antonio is a nice man.'

'I know him. He came on a few diving expeditions with Dimitri and I, and I liked him... But I am not such a nice man...'

'Oh, I wouldn't say that. Antonio is a friend— nothing more. You were my lover.'

'I don't like the past tense.'

Should she take a chance and tell Rion the truth? Well, she had nothing to lose. 'Remember when you suggested extending our cruise, I wanted to say yes.'

Rion tensed, his long fingers digging into her waist as his other hand moved to cup her chin. 'You did? Then why…?' There was confusion in the dark eyes that held hers, and something else that made her heart leap in her breast.

Selina took a deep breath. 'Remember the night I left your bed and told you the next day it was because I had almost fallen out? Well, it wasn't true. That was the night I realised I had fallen in love with you again. I also realised with our shared past it was hopeless. I saw no point in prolonging the trip for a few more days because that was all it could ever be. Plus I was frightened I'd let slip what Bratchet was really like, and I didn't trust you not to tell him. Stupid, really. I ended up telling you anyway.'

'You said you loved me?' Rion stared fixedly at her and she was struck dumb at the emotion she saw in his eyes. 'You humble me,' he rasped. 'I know I can't expect you to still love me after the way I have behaved, and I can't blame you for not trusting me—I have done precious little to earn your trust. But I swear if you will give me another chance and marry me I will spend every day for the rest of my life trying to win your love and trust.' He kissed her lightly, almost reverently, on the lips, taking a step back to set her free.

Selina stood in the middle of the bedroom, emotion at his words blocking her throat. She swallowed hard and searched his face for the truth. The rigidity of his features was betrayed by a muscle pulsing under the tanned skin. Her golden eyes met his and she saw his heart in his eyes, the mask of arrogance stripped away to reveal the vulnerable man beneath. She believed him, and yet she was still nervous.

'Are you really sure about this…us…?'

'I was never more certain of anything in my life. And if you still don't believe me—tough.' The vulnerable penitent gone, he reached for her and swung her up in his arms and onto the bed, pinned her beneath him. 'I will have to convince you—in my defence, I love you.'

'Wait…' But he bent his dark head and took her mouth with a hard, hungry kiss that sent liq-

uid fire flowing through her veins, and Selina
wrapped her arms around him and gave in to
the inevitable magic of his touch.

'I worship you, Selina,' he groaned staring down into her wide, gleaming gold eyes.
'Everything that you are—funny, caring, com-
passionate, with a heart like a lion, beautiful
inside and out. My life is meaningless without
you,' he told her throatily, his mouth grazing
hers again.

Between kisses and caresses he stripped off
their clothes, and with his great body half covering her they kissed—a slow, deep kiss full of
promises of love and passion that made Selina's
heart tremble. Lost in the wonder of his love,
with eager hands she caressed his powerful
body, her eyes closing in ecstasy as Rion wor-
shipped every inch of her with hands and mouth
and husky words of love, until finally they were
one in every way—heart, body and soul.

Selina stirred happily in the protective curve
of Rion's arm and glanced around. Pulling herself up on one elbow, she looked down at him.

'Do you really own this hotel or did you just say that to shut me up?' she asked with a grin, stroking her hand across his broad chest.

Rion groaned and caught her hand in his. 'Yes, I'd never lie to you. I own quite a few properties in the centres of major cities—they are a good investment.'

She hid a smile. The tycoon was talking. Then she remembered. 'You told me that before. I should thank you for keeping quiet,' she said seriously. 'Bratchet did go back to Cambodia, and he was arrested, but he couldn't bribe his way out of it this time and his trial is in a few months' time in America.'

'That's great.' Rion's eyes hardened for an instant. He already knew. By contacting the right, if not the most law-abiding, people he had made sure of it. Where bribery was concerned there was always a higher bidder. It was not something he ever did, but with Bratchet he had made an exception. But with Selina, the woman he loved, sprawled naked over his chest he wasn't about to tell her and spoil the moment. 'I dropped out of the deal when you dropped out of my life.'

And, wrapping a hand around the back of her head, he kissed her and showed her all over again how much he loved her.

A long time later she opened her eyes to see Rion staring down at her, a wary expression on his handsome face. 'What?' she asked languorously.

'You have not said yes, you will marry me.'

Selina burst out laughing. 'I don't think you ever asked. You simply told me.'

'So *will* you marry me—again?'

'Yes.'

He kissed her brow, a decidedly smug smile on his face, and smoothed back the tangled mass of hair from her face.

'But I am thinking I don't want to get married—'

'What?' Rion exclaimed.

'Let me finish.' She grinned. 'I was going to say *in Greece*—because I had no luck last time.

I would like it to be just the two of us at a registry office in England.'

'Fine.' Rion heaved a deep breath, his moment of panic over. 'I will arrange it as soon as we get back—and this time will be different, I promise. No more working sixteen-hour days.'

Suddenly Selina wasn't so sure she was doing the right thing. It had all happened so fast. And Rion had swept her off her feet once before.

'I'll believe that when I see it—and what about the other women?' she blurted, memories of the past coming back to haunt her.

Rion's mouth tightened. He was not accustomed to explaining his behaviour to anyone, but he realised if he had talked or listened to Selina in the beginning he would never have lost her, and if he wanted to win Selina's trust again he had to be one-hundred-percent honest with her.

'From the moment I set eyes on you I never looked at another woman until long after the divorce.'

'I find that hard to believe. The night we met, you didn't have a conference call—you had a date with a woman called Chloe. Iris showed me the picture. Though I'm surprised Chloe only gave you four out of ten for performance,' she couldn't help teasing.

'Iris showed you too damn much,' he snorted. 'I did have a date with Chloe and I intended taking her to bed. Is that what you want to hear? But after I met you I took her to a club, took her home and left her at the door. She was angry because I *didn't* take her to bed—a woman scorned... As for the others—I didn't even know them. And the reason I worked so much when we were married was because your grandfather was a crafty old villain. The deal was my father's, but after it went through my father took off on his cruise and asked me to sort it out. Stakis Shipping was in a much worse state than had been presented to him and it took me three months to save the damn thing from going bust.'

'Oh no! Though, knowing my grandfather, I can believe that,' she said. And with a questioning look she added, 'But you did know about the deal, because you married me.'

'Why are we talking about this now? Yes, my father asked me, and I gave him an emphatic no. But to humour him I went to the dinner, and you know the rest.'

'Yes, you thought you'd got me pregnant.'

'I took one look at you and wanted you, and after we made love I thought you might be pregnant. It only took one look six years later for me to want you just as badly—more so. In fact I think I loved you all along. But finding a man in your bed so enraged me I blocked you from my mind. It was the only way I could deal with the fury I felt. And I have carried on working sixteen-hour days ever since, so that should tell you something.' He tightened his arm around Selina. He wasn't going to lose her now.

'What about Lydia? Iris said you were still in love with her?'

Rion chuckled. 'You're jealous—that is what this is all about—and trust me you have no need to be. You remember the woman Lydia was with when I introduced you? That is her lover—has been for years.' He told Selina the whole story.

'But she is *married*,' Selina said, round-eyed with amazement.

'You are still so naive in some ways.' He chuckled. 'Lydia would have married *any* man. There had been the odd rumour about her sexual preferences, and her parents are the strict high-society types. She could never come out as a lesbian. That is why she married Bastias. He is old enough and flattered enough to have got her and Lydia can get away with anything. She is a nice woman. I have known her since I was about twelve and we've stayed friends. The reason I was arguing with the paparazzi guy was that he was asking Lydia awkward questions about her girlfriend, who was actually standing behind us at the time.'

Selina laughed, feeling mightily relieved. 'My, what a colourful life you lead, Rion.'

'Well, you have heard about mine, but I won't ask you about yours. It is enough to know you are mine now,' Rion declared huskily.

'You know all there is to tell. I have only had one lover—you.'

Rion stared at her. 'But you were taking the Pill.'

'Yes, a low-dose one for cramps.'

Rion reached for her head and threaded his fingers through her hair, held her face firmly in his hands. 'I think I am dreaming.' The pupils of his eyes darkened, dilating with passion. 'You are everything in the world to me, Selina, and I will treasure you to my dying day and beyond.' And with a groan he covered her mouth with his, kissing her with a depth of passion and pure love.

Selina held her baby son in her arms unable to take her eyes off him. He was so gorgeous, with black hair just like his father.

'Smile for the camera, Selina,' Rion ordered, and she did tear her gaze away from her child— for her husband.

'How many is that?' She laughed.

Rion grinned. 'A lot.' He moved to the bedside and kissed her. 'Have I told you today I love you?' He kissed her again. 'And I thank you with all my heart for our beautiful son.' His dark eyes suspiciously moist, he gazed at the baby in her arms. 'I never imagined in my wildest dreams such happiness existed, and it is all down to you, my love.'

'My turn, Daddy. I want to see my brother,' a little voice piped up.

Rion chuckled and picked up a little girl with red-gold hair and amber eyes—the image of her mother. 'And so you shall, my heart.' He kissed the child and sat down on the side of the bed, holding two-year-old Phoebe. 'There—now you can kiss his cheek and say hello to Theodore.'

Phoebe pursed her lips and gave the baby a big kiss. 'Hello, Theodore.' She sat on her daddy's knee, silently watching the baby for a while, then with a big sigh said, 'He doesn't talk, and he is too tiny to play with me.' She looked at Selina and said, 'Can we go home now, Mummy?' Their live-wire daughter was already bored.

Rion looked at Selina and they both burst out laughing.

'You and Daddy can, as it is nearly your bedtime, but your brother and I have to stay the night. We will be home in the morning,' Selina replied to her beloved daughter, and after a few hugs and kisses—one passionate one for Selina from Rion—she watched them depart.

Alone with her son, she let a smile of pure happiness curve her full lips. Her free hand went as it so often did to the pendant around her neck. Rion had given it to her on their second wedding night and told her he had bought it for her nineteenth birthday. Their initials were entwined in diamonds on a platinum chain. He'd also told her he had planned a honeymoon to the Seychelles for the following week, when Iris would have been back at school. But as they'd never made it he was taking no chances and they were going to the Caribbean this time.

She loved him more than ever, and was beginning to believe he might have loved her from the start.

Surprisingly Beth was convinced of it. Had been ever since Selina had arrived in Cambodia from her stay on Rion's yacht. A large donation had arrived on the same day as Selina, and Beth had winkled the truth out of her. Beth had become a champion of Rion and now they were all great friends. So much so that Trevor and Beth were Phoebe's godparents.

Contrary to what he had once said, Rion was a very jealous and possessive man. He had bought her another Mercedes a week after they'd got back together. She had tried to object, and laughed when he'd told her he didn't like the idea that a friend had bought her a car any more than he'd liked a drunk being in her bed. He'd said if it was him even blind drunk he would still be aware she was in his bed...

She had told him she had bought the car herself, and the 'friend' with her had been the elderly gentleman who lived next door. Though he would never admit it, Rion had looked relieved.

The past four years had seen all her dreams come true, she thought happily. Their main home was a beautiful house in the hills high above Athens that Rion had had an architect design and build to his specifications. He had given his stepmother, Helen, the old home. They also had a house in London, and a holiday home in the Caribbean, and of course the villa on Letos, greatly renovated now, which Anna still looked after.

Rion rarely worked long hours, and had cut his trips abroad to the minimum. If it was possible Selina and Phoebe went with him. Rion adored Phoebe and was a very hands-on father, playing with her, bathing her. But then again he was a very hands-on husband, she thought. Rarely a day passed when he didn't make love to her, and she knew with absolute certainty that he loved her.

A nurse walked in and took her son to put him in the crib by her bed, telling her to get some sleep.

With a smile on her face Selina curled up on her side and watched her sleeping baby until her eyes closed and she fell asleep.

A slight noise woke her up, and immediately she glanced at the baby. But it wasn't the baby, it was Rion. He sat down on the bed.

'What are you doing here?' she whispered. 'What time is it?'

'After ten. Don't worry. Phoebe is asleep and Aunt Peggy is watching over her.' Leaning forward, he put a hand either side of Selina on the bed. 'It is her father that needs you,' he said huskily. He brushed her lips lightly, then kissed her deeply. 'I couldn't go to bed without saying goodnight.' He nuzzled her throat and the baby whimpered.

The nurse walked in, smiled, but told Rion to leave. With another kiss for Selina, for once Rion did as he was told and left.

'You are a lucky woman. That man worships the ground you walk on,' said the nurse.

'I know.' Selina smiled and, totally secure in his love, she did know.

* * * * *

Mills & Boon® Large Print

August 2012

A DEAL AT THE ALTAR
Lynne Graham

RETURN OF THE MORALIS WIFE
Jacqueline Baird

GIANNI'S PRIDE
Kim Lawrence

UNDONE BY HIS TOUCH
Annie West

THE CATTLE KING'S BRIDE
Margaret Way

NEW YORK'S FINEST REBEL
Trish Wylie

THE MAN WHO SAW HER BEAUTY
Michelle Douglas

THE LAST REAL COWBOY
Donna Alward

THE LEGEND OF DE MARCO
Abby Green

STEPPING OUT OF THE SHADOWS
Robyn Donald

DESERVING OF HIS DIAMONDS?
Melanie Milburne

0712 Rom LP

Mills & Boon® Large Print

September 2012

A VOW OF OBLIGATION
Lynne Graham

DEFYING DRAKON
Carole Mortimer

PLAYING THE GREEK'S GAME
Sharon Kendrick

ONE NIGHT IN PARADISE
Maisey Yates

VALTIERI'S BRIDE
Caroline Anderson

THE NANNY WHO KISSED HER BOSS
Barbara McMahon

FALLING FOR MR MYSTERIOUS
Barbara Hannay

THE LAST WOMAN HE'D EVER DATE
Liz Fielding

HIS MAJESTY'S MISTAKE
Jane Porter

DUTY AND THE BEAST
Trish Morey

THE DARKEST OF SECRETS
Kate Hewitt